5/98

MILE-HIGH LOVE

MILE-HIGH LOVE

•

Jane McBride Choate

AVALON BOOKS
THOMAS BOUREGY AND COMPANY, INC.
401 LAFAYETTE STREET
NEW YORK, NEW YORK 10003

© Copyright 1998 by Jane McBride Choate
Library of Congress Catalog Card Number 98-96071
ISBN 0-8034-9297-9

PRINTED IN THE UNITED STATES OF AMERICA
ON ACID-FREE PAPER
BY HADDON CRAFTSMEN, BLOOMSBURG, PENNSYLVANIA

To Marian Quakenbush and Tami McClure, walking buddies and friends who do their best to keep me in shape.

Chapter One

*B*uckles and Bows. The name in gold script above the door of her Denver shop always made Miranda Kirk smile. Even after three years. The vintage clothing boutique was a dream come true. For five years she'd worked for someone else, learning and storing it away. When the opportunity had come to open her own place, she'd jumped at it and hadn't looked back.

Denver's infamous brown cloud of smog hovered over the skyline, blurring the backdrop of mountain and sky. It didn't dim her pleasure in the day, though. Smog was a small price to pay for living in the Mile-High state.

Fall had painted the trees in the gaudy colors of autumn—scarlet and amber, saffron and ocher. The air

1

smelled of burning leaves and the deeper, richer scent of the mountains.

She loved this small pocket of the city with its vigor, its diversity, its contrasts. Thrift shops flanked expensive boutiques. Country western bars rubbed shoulders with pizzerias. She could order spicy Thai chicken for lunch and calzone for dinner, both within the same block. Slowly, she and others like her were reclaiming this piece of the city.

Renamed the Aspen Heights district, the area was attracting a lot of publicity from other parts of the city anxious to do the same thing.

The people looked out for each other, weaving a close-knit community that older residents claimed was reminiscent of the fifties. People knew their neighbors' names and used them. They invited each other to baptisms and bar mitzvahs, christenings and funerals. They celebrated together at Greek festivals and Jewish Hanukkahs, traditional weddings and not-so-traditional ones.

The solid middle-class neighborhood had taken its share of knocks during the seventies, disintegrated further in the eighties until it was home to only drug pushers and their clientele by the early nineties. The last few years had seen a change.

First one enterprising family, unable to afford a house in the suburbs, had bought a fixer-upper. Others had followed. Houses built following World War II now sported fresh paint jobs and swept stoops, flower beds and manicured yards. Ethnic markets and craft shops replaced abandoned stores.

This was home to her. But this morning her mind was on other things. Her mother, to be exact. After eighteen years as a widow, Holly Kirk was remarrying. Miranda was happy for her mother, but worry slipped through her pleasure. Her mother had never shown any interest in a man since the death of her husband. Now she was planning to marry a man she'd known less than six months.

Miranda pushed aside her worry as she slipped the key in the lock and went inside.

It took a moment for what she saw to register. When it did, a gasp broke from her lips. Antique brooches were scattered with Native-American necklaces. Silver shoe buckles were mixed with Art Deco bangles. Earrings rested on their sides or facedown. Vintage clothing, rich with lace and brocade, was strewn across the floor.

She'd been robbed. The idea wouldn't penetrate. It made no sense. Sure, she knew about the other burglaries in the area, but she hadn't believed it would happen to her. Her store didn't carry the pricey items that some of the other stores in the area did.

The boutique was her pride and joy. It was also her livelihood. She scoured flea markets, auctions, and estate sales, looking for bits and treasures from bygone years to replenish her stock. Seeing the devastation was a blow to the gut that nearly doubled her over.

She should get out of here, she thought. Hadn't she been told that if a place had been robbed, you should get out fast and go somewhere—anywhere—else to call 911 in case the burglar was still there? She did just that.

By the time she'd called the police from the store next door, she was shaking. Overriding the fear, though, was anger.

Deep, abiding anger.

Detective Lieutenant MacKenzie Torrence had downed enough coffee during the last twenty-four hours to keep him awake for the next seven days. He was wired. A hot meal, a shower, and about three solid days' sleep, and he might just start to feel human again.

A call from the captain to take the call at some store called Buckles and Bows had him groaning. He had already put in double shifts, but the department was shorthanded, with nearly one-third of the force out with the flu after a particularly virulent strain had hit Denver.

He gave a weary sigh. He was definitely getting too old for these kinds of hours. The thought made him sigh again. He was tired of a lot of things—like coming home every night to an empty apartment and an even emptier life.

Lately he'd caught himself wondering what it would be like actually to have a private life. To have something more besides work and more work to fill the days and the nights, to have a real home with a wife and children.

There'd been a time when he'd razzed the men who rushed home after their shifts, eager to kiss their wives and play with their kids. No station wagon and picket fence for him; he valued his freedom too much. But times had changed.

He had changed.

He arrived at Buckles and Bows within five minutes of receiving the call. A uniformed officer was there waiting. His young, eager face reminded Mac of himself fifteen years ago. A rookie, fresh out of the academy, he'd been sure he was going to single-handedly save the world.

Since then, he'd learned that all he could do was chip away at the violence that plagued his city. It was a city much like others, with its share of problems and ills—gangs, drugs, and poverty. All that kept him going sometimes was the belief that he was making a difference. Lately he was beginning to doubt even that. And that scared him more than any punk with a gun.

"Detective?" The fresh-faced rookie gave Mac a diffident smile. "Markham."

Mac spared a moment to shake the man's hand. "Torrence. Burglary. Have you figured out when it happened?"

"Owner claims the shop was locked up tight when she left last night."

"When would that be?"

"Six-thirty."

"So we can narrow the time down to somewhere between when she closed up and this morning. How'd they get in?"

"Same as the others. A high-tech job. They by-passed the security system without triggering the alarm." Markham pointed to the professional manner in which the burglary alarm had been disarmed.

A string of burglaries had hit the district, drawing outrage from the local businesspeople. Mac didn't blame them. So far the perp hadn't left a single clue, and the cops were no closer to solving the crimes than they were over a month ago when the first one had occurred.

He gave the shop a once-over from the outside. Nice enough. The neighborhood had recently been gentrified—old houses bought up by young families, once-abandoned stores turned into trendy boutiques and bistros.

"What's your make on the owner?" he asked the rookie.

"Youngish. Pretty." The sudden flare in Markham's

eyes told Mac she was a great deal more than merely pretty. "She's upset, naturally. Mad at us for letting it happen."

Mac shrugged. Victims frequently took out their anger on the cops. The perps were long gone, leaving the boys in blue to take the heat.

Making sure he didn't touch the doorknob, he walked inside. A pretty blond was waiting for him. She was small, barely five feet, with a slight build. The owner, he supposed, though she looked barely out of her teens.

Until he looked closer. Then he saw the determined lift of her chin, the proud bearing that said she might bend, but wouldn't break. The brown eyes that met his were troubled. There was something else as well. Anger. Unless he missed his guess, the lady was mad as heck.

It interested him.

Her features were soft, almost elegant, in a face that might have posed for one of Botticelli's angels. Delicate, he decided, until he looked at the set of her jaw. There was toughness there, a determination that belied the otherwise fragile air.

He wasn't much on women's clothing styles, but he noted that her fitted suit and silk blouse were different from the usual fare. Softer and more feminine, like something from another era. He'd always been a sucker for the old-fashioned look.

He stuck out his hand. "Detective Torrence."

She put her hand in his. "Miranda Kirk." Her hand was like the woman herself: small but with an underlying strength.

The spark of interest that stirred within him was as unexpected as it was unwelcome. He had a job to do. His gaze swept the room, taking in the scattered clothing and jewelry, the overturned cash register. It returned to the woman, and he frowned at the pallor of her skin.

"Are you all right?" he asked.

"I'm fine." The clipped tone of her voice suggested that the question had annoyed her.

There'd be bruises tomorrow, he guessed shrewdly. Emotional ones that didn't show. Victims of burglaries lost more than material goods. They lost their security, their trust in people and the basic goodness of the world. It was a hard lesson.

There he went again. Focusing on the woman instead of the job. The jolt of attraction he felt disturbed him. It made his voice sharper than he'd intended. "What time did you arrive this morning?"

"A little after nine. We open at ten."

"You didn't notice anything out of place outside? Something that didn't seem right?"

"No."

"How much did they get?"

"A little over fifty dollars from the petty cash drawer."

He raised his brows. "Do you usually keep more cash than that on hand?"

She shook her head. "I make a deposit at the bank every evening. And if they, whoever they are, had an ounce of sense, they'd have known it. Aren't the bad guys supposed to case the joint?"

Mac hid a grin. The pretty lady was talking like something from a B-grade movie. He scribbled something in his notebook and nodded. "Anything else?"

"Some necklaces and rings." She nodded toward the jewelry cases. "I don't carry much of the real stuff. Mostly costume pieces. I can't afford to buy the more expensive pieces outright. So I take them on consignment."

"What about the other things in the shop?"

"The vintage clothing I pick up at estate sales, thrift stores, a few from private sales."

Mac picked up a chain and let it run through his fingers. "Looks like the real thing."

"It's very well crafted. But it's imitation."

"That looks like gold." He pointed to several necklaces tossed over a black velvet backdrop.

She shook her head. "Gold plate. He took the most valuable things and left the others. Nothing that I carry, though, is worth enough to warrant this." Her voice cracked on the last word. She flicked a glance his way, and he braced himself. But her next words weren't the expected rebuke.

"How long does it usually take for cases like this one to be solved?"

Markham had joined them by now. The two officers exchanged glances. "It depends," Mac said at last.

"On what?"

"If there are any witnesses or if we can collect any evidence, like fingerprints."

"I see."

Markhan nodded and turned to go, but at the door he stopped and looked back. "Does your shop have a layaway plan?"

"Not usually. But sometimes I'll make a special arrangement with a customer. Why do you ask?"

"I was just thinking my mother would like that brooch." He pointed to an Art Deco piece. "Her birthday's coming up real soon."

Her eyes softened, and she smiled. "Come in anytime. I'm sure we'll be able to work something out." The smile was still on her face when she turned back to Mac.

"Very nice," he said, eyeing the brooch. The piece wasn't Tiffany quality, but it was still pricey. He doubted a beat cop had the money to afford the shop's merchandise. "You know, of course, that he can't afford that."

"I'll make sure he can." The quiet determination in her voice told him she'd do just that.

"Must not make a lot of money that way," he commented.

"I do all right."

He looked around the shop. Even with the clutter and disarray, he could see that she carried quality stuff. "I'm sure you do." He eyed her outfit. "Is what you're wearing something from here?"

Her expression momentarily lightened. "Yes. Do you like it?"

"Very much." His words came out as a croak, and he cleared his throat, reminding himself he was here to do a job. "I have to ask you some more questions."

She shut her eyes and drew a deep breath, then another. Then she opened her eyes. "All right."

He crossed the room to lean against the front counter.

For a big man, he moved with athletic grace, she noted.

"Has anything unusual happened in the last week or two? Any strangers come into the shop, someone who looked like he didn't belong?"

She considered his question, itching to straighten up the mess and knowing she had better not touch anything until the place had been gone over by the lab team who had arrived only minutes earlier. She hadn't been a cop's daughter for nothing. "No. We have a pretty regular clientele. There's the occasional tourist, but mostly we cater to the same people.''

"Anyone who didn't fit in with the normal customers?''

She thought about it. "No. Just the usual.''

"Had any repair work done?''

She shook her head.

"What about your house?''

"I'm having some concrete poured for a patio.''

"I suppose you checked their references.''

Did he think she was a complete idiot? "Of course I checked. They're the best. Maybe you ought to be out chasing down leads instead of giving me the third degree.'' Defensiveness narrowed her eyes and sharpened her voice.

"Hey, I'm not the bad guy here,'' he said.

Immediately she felt ashamed. "I'm sorry. It's been a hard morning.''

"I wasn't questioning your judgment. I'm just looking for something—anything—that might give me a clue about who did this. Does anyone besides you have access to the store after hours?''

"Just the cleaning service.''

"How long have you used them?''

"Ever since I opened. Three years ago.'' She thought of the Dominguez family, who'd approached her the very day she'd opened. They'd presented references, but that wasn't what had persuaded her to hire them. It had been the quiet but unmistakable air of love she'd sensed between the parents and the children.

Her instincts hadn't betrayed her. The Dominguezes had proven to be hard workers with a determination to make a better life for themselves that continued to amaze her.

"You're not planning on questioning them, are you? Where they came from . . . the police were the enemy."

He'd heard of such things, of course. That wasn't the issue now.

"None of them would hurt me, but you're just going to have to take my word for it. They deserve their privacy."

In the three years since she'd opened Buckles and Bows, she'd had no complaint about the Dominguezes' work and had recommended them to friends who ran a boutique specializing in wearable art.

"It's SOP," he said.

Standard operating procedure. How often had she heard her father use that same phrase?

The Dominguez family had endured a lifetime of poverty and hardship before leaving their home in Central America and coming to the United States. After making sure the children—five of them—had passed the citizenship test, the parents were now studying for their own.

Miranda had a special liking for the youngest boy in the family, Juan. He had the face of an angel. But it was more than that. He wanted so much. He was always struggling, striving for something more. Like the older kids, he worked for the family business. But he wouldn't be content there forever.

She knew it. She suspected he knew it as well. He was too eager, too hungry to be satisfied working for someone else—even family. He'd make his mark someday. She only hoped she'd be there to see it.

"The Dominguezes had nothing to do with it," she said again, bringing herself back to the present.

Mac looked like he wanted to argue, but he simply shook his head. "You may like them, but you can't afford to take chances."

"I'm not," she said quietly. "Not with the Dominguezes. They're friends."

As far as she was concerned, that said it all. Her friendship with the family was precious, and she didn't intend to jeopardize it.

"They're pretty lucky," Mac observed quietly. "Having you as a friend."

The obvious sincerity in his voice warmed her. As did the admiration in his eyes. She was fast in danger of letting herself be charmed, much as she disliked the idea.

Mac exhaled a long breath and plowed a hand through his hair. Shadows underscored gray, heavily fringed eyes. He looked tired, she thought with a rush of sympathy. Tired and discouraged. She recognized the symptoms. She'd seen them often enough in her father.

"How long have you been up, Detective Torrence?"

He looked surprised at the question but answered readily enough. "Going on thirty-six hours. And it's Mac." At her raised eyebrows, he added, "Short for MacKenzie."

"Do you always work double shifts . . . Mac?"

That drew a faint smile from him. "No. Only when the bad guys do."

"Would you like some coffee? Or tea?"

"I wouldn't say no to a cup of coffee."

She went to the back room and returned with two steaming cups a few minutes later. "It's instant," she apologized as she handed him a mug.

"Doesn't matter," he said after taking a sip. "You probably saved my life." He finished the coffee and straightened. "There's not much more I can do until we get a report from the lab boys." He looked about and spotted a computer. "Can you get me an inventory of what was taken?"

"Sure." She booted up the computer and pushed a couple of buttons. The printer spit out several sheets of paper within a few seconds. After looking the list over and checking off the obvious items, she handed the papers to him.

"Great."

"Detective, what are the chances of catching whoever did this?"

"Truth?"

"Please."

"Unless we get lucky and the techs come up with something . . ." His shrug said the rest.

She drew a breath, then let it out in a heavy sigh. She'd known the answer before she'd even voiced the question.

"Detective?" One of the lab team tapped him on the shoulder.

Mac turned to confer with him and then turned back to her. "We're almost through. We managed to lift a few prints from the glass cases, so we're going to have to fingerprint you and see what's left."

"I understand."

"We expected to find more than the couple of sets of prints," he said.

"The cleaning crew comes in every evening after I close."

He nodded. "Well, that'll make things a little easier if we can eliminate customers."

The next few minutes were spent taking her fingerprints. She washed the ink from her hands and tried to ignore the warmth left by the feeling of his hands upon hers.

"I'd best be shoving off," he said.

"You're leaving?" Only minutes before, she'd wanted him gone, impatient with his questions and his attitude. But now that he was about to leave, she was reluctant to see him go.

Where were her fine courage and nerve and self-sufficiency now? Where was the independence that had allowed her to start her own business when all the odds were against her?

He gave her a shrewd look. "Would you like me to stay?"

"No," she said quickly. Too quickly. "I mean, it's not like they're going to come back or anything." The last came out as a question, and she realized she was holding her breath, waiting. For reassurance, she supposed. Reassurance and a promise that it wouldn't happen again. She recognized the latter as unrealistic. It didn't stop her from wanting it, though.

"Probably not," he agreed.

She'd have preferred a more positive answer, but she nodded, appreciating his honesty. "You'll let me know if you hear anything?"

"You can count on it." He hesitated a moment before reaching out to touch her arm, his hand warm and comforting. "I'll ask the patrols to make a couple of extra pass-bys . . . just in case."

"Thanks."

She had to close the store, of course. The lab boys had come and gone, giving her the go-ahead to begin cleaning up the mess.

Suzanne Brockway, Miranda's assistant and friend, breezed in just as the detective left. "Who's the hunk?" She didn't give Miranda a chance to answer the question as she looked around. "What's going on?"

"The hunk's a detective. And we were robbed."

"Are you all right?"

"I'm fine." That was a lie, of course.

Apparently Suzanne saw through it, for she curved an arm around Miranda's shoulders and hugged her. "I hope they catch the creep who did this. And when they do, I'm going to . . ."

Suzanne described what she had in mind in vivid detail, her suggestions growing more outrageous with every moment until Miranda began to feel sorry for the thief if Suzanne ever met up with him.

"I don't think that's legal anymore," she said at her friend's last idea of tarring and feathering the burglar.

"It should be."

Miranda knew her friend was trying to take her mind off the destruction around her. "Thanks."

Twenty-two years old, Suzanne was a grad student working to put herself through school. Not for the first time, Miranda wondered at their friendship. Physically, they couldn't be more different. Suzanne was knock-dead gorgeous. Long hair—red, today—and emerald green eyes, courtesy of contact lenses, highlighted perfect features. Her lush curves on a five-foot-ten-inch frame drew more whistles than a train crossing.

Her hair changed color almost as frequently as she changed outfits. She favored leggings, oversize tops, and dangling earrings. Today she wore an orange-and-hot-pink sweater over turquoise tights. Purple high-tops tied with neon green laces completed the look. The effect should have been jarring. But Suzanne carried it off with panache.

Miranda, at five foot nothing, always felt like a drab sparrow next to a vivid peacock. Beneath Suzanne's bright plumage, though, lay a warm and tender heart.

Despite their differences or perhaps because of them, the two women had become firm friends. When Miranda had needed an assistant at Buckles and Bows, she'd placed an ad in the help wanted section of the paper, and Suzanne had answered it.

They listened to each other's hopes and dreams, problems and fears. Miranda had never been more grateful for her friend than she was right now.

"Let's see what that low-life scum did." Eyes wide, Suzanne looked about, crying a bit when she saw that some of the clothing had been damaged. She picked up an evening gown from the fifties. The straps had been ripped and the bodice torn.

A robe in pure white, trimmed with boa feathers, lay crumpled in a heap. Circa 1930, it was one of her favorites, a vampy bit of satin and silk that made her think of scarlet-lipped movie stars and romantic classics.

"What kind of pig does this kind of thing?" Suzanne asked, her voice tear-husky.

There was no answer to that. None that made sense. "Why don't you go on home?" Miranda suggested. "We can't open today."

"I'll stay and help you clean up."

Miranda shook her head. "I have to call the insurance agency and have them send someone out." After a few minutes, she'd persuaded Suzanne to go home.

"I'll be here early tomorrow," her friend promised.

Miranda laughed for the first time since she'd walked into the store. Reluctantly, Suzanne joined in. Her assistant had a long-standing habit of arriving late.

Miranda spent the rest of the day filling out forms for the insurance company and cleaning up after the fingerprint team. Sorting through the clothes took much longer. Silks and satins, furs and sequins. Each item had to be assessed to determine whether it needed to be cleaned or repaired. Cleaning such fragile garments wasn't a simple matter of taking them to the dry cleaner's. Vintage clothes required special care, available only at a handful of cleaners.

The number of items requiring repairs continued to grow. Each item she placed on the pile would eat into her profits. She was grateful for something specific to keep her occupied.

Unfortunately, she still had too much time to think. Too much time to wonder at her reaction to the handsome detective. Too much time to remember how his hand had felt upon her own.

Definitely too much time.

Chapter Two

Mac had little to report when he returned to Buckles and Bows the following morning.

Three additional officers had called in sick, leaving the precinct more shorthanded than ever. The captain had added two more cases to Mac's already heavy caseload. But he'd emphasized that the burglaries in the Aspen Heights district were to receive precedence.

"The mayor and city council are coming down hard on the department," the captain had said in an early morning briefing. "The area's supposed to be a showplace, a model of what concerned citizens and the city fathers can do together."

Much as he wanted to see the lovely Ms. Kirk again, Mac had other cases, more important ones, that needed his attention. He said as much, earning a frown from his commander.

"Let the uniforms handle it," he said. "We need high visibility. The mayor wants the best on this. That's you."

Mac had heard all the rhetoric before. Police work was becoming more about pleasing the politicians than protecting the people.

It wasn't the first time he'd disagreed with the brass. It wouldn't be the last. He was a professional. And that meant he would do his job, whatever his feelings.

"You're the hunk," a sultry voice said, bringing him back to the present.

He turned and did a double take. The woman had wildly curling hair that tumbled below her waist. Four gold loops studded each ear. A scarlet-and-purple jumpsuit outlined every inch of a body that could— and probably did—stop traffic.

"Detective Torrence," he said, holding out his hand.

She didn't so much put her hand in his as she draped it on top of his. "Suzanne Brockway. I work for Miranda."

"I didn't see you yesterday." He grinned. "I would have remembered."

She gave him an appreciative smile. "I was late."

"Your boss around?"

''Right here.'' Miranda stepped out from the back office, a candy bar in her hand.

The assistant, Mac thought, was a knockout, but it was the owner who held his interest. The smile that slid across his lips had nothing to do with seeing her again, he assured himself. Nothing at all.

She was wearing one of those softly fitted suits again, this one in a dark blue that made her skin seem creamier than ever. The white blouse had a floppy bow at the neck. An excuse of a hat sat at a cocky angle on her softly waving hair, a wisp of a veil teasing her forehead. It was a look that wouldn't work on every woman. On this one, it was sensational.

She looked as fresh as one of the flowers crowded into a fat crock atop the counter. But her attitude said ''Keep out.''

Ladylike suits and a standoffish attitude. An irresistible combination.

''I thought you might close the store for another day,'' he said.

Her chin came up at that. ''You thought wrong.''

The lady had guts. More than her share, he thought. She'd been through a burglary, an experience that would have devastated most people, and she had opened the store anyway.

He dragged his thoughts back to the job.

Her eyes asked the question before her lips formed the word. ''Any news?''

He shook his head. "We've come up with a big fat zero. That's why I'm back. I need to ask you some more questions." I'm going to need the names and addresses of your cleaning crew, the men pouring concrete—"

"What about me?" Suzanne asked in a husky voice.

Mac grinned again. "You too, Miss Brockway."

"Suzanne."

The kid was younger than his baby sister. He felt like an old man compared to her. He recognized a practiced flirt and gave her an indulgent smile. "I appreciate your cooperation."

"Anytime, Detective." She gave him another one of those come-hither smiles, guaranteed to a turn a man inside out.

"I'll let you two discuss the case," Suzanne said with a wink and sauntered off.

Miranda watched while Suzanne strutted her stuff in front of Mac. His eyes had widened a bit as she sashayed her way across the room, the jumpsuit stretching to accommodate her every move.

The man wouldn't be human if he didn't react to the vision before him. To his credit, he didn't drool. Men had been known to do so when confronted with Suzanne's obvious charms.

She knew Suzanne flirted as easily as she breathed and that it meant nothing.

"She's a cute kid," Mac said when Suzanne was out of earshot.

Kid? "She likes you."

"She's just practicing on me. Besides, she's too old for me."

A smile came to Miranda's lips. So the cop had a sense of humor. A handy trait. Especially when you had to confront the realities of crime on a daily basis. One experience was plenty for her.

Her smile died. She'd learned enough from her father to know that the longer a case went unsolved, the greater the likelihood that it would remain that way.

Mac was having a hard time concentrating on anything but the shape of Miranda's mouth. She had the softest-looking lips he'd ever seen. Fleetingly, he wondered how they would feel, what they would taste like, pressed against his own. Her scent, soap-and-water fresh, wafted through the air.

The case.

He had to concentrate on the case. With an effort, he dragged his thoughts back to the investigation and gave himself a mental shake. He was a cop, a good one, but he was acting like the greenest of rookies fresh out of the academy, mooning over a pretty face.

"I'd like to ask you some more questions." He gestured to the chair.

Did she have any enemies?

Had she fired any employees during the last year?

Had she had any disagreements over payment with any of her consignees?

No.

No.

No.

The questions were standard, but he sensed her impatience.

"I don't have anything more to add," she said.

"Sometimes you can know things that you aren't even aware of. I'd like you to think about it. Maybe you'll remember something." He reached into his jacket pocket and produced a card. "You have my office number. I'll give you my home number too." He scrawled a number on it and handed it to her. "Don't hesitate to call if you think of something. Anything at all. Even if you don't think it's important."

She glanced at the card, noting the strong, angular slant of his writing, then laid it on her desk.

He took a moment to trail a finger down the softly draping bow at her neck. "Pretty."

"Thanks." He watched as her face flushed pink. "I bought it here."

"You have to buy your own stuff?"

That earned a smile from her. "You bet. This is a business."

"It suits you."

Miranda narrowed her eyes, not liking the warmth spreading through her at his words. Still, she couldn't quite quash the instant bloom of feminine pleasure at the fact that he'd noticed what she wore. She had no interest in the man, she reminded herself. Still, good manners required that she acknowledge the compliment. ''Thanks.''

''You're welcome.'' He took off shortly after that.

The detective managed to intrude upon her thoughts to an annoying degree for the rest of the day. Suzanne's teasing didn't help matters.

''The hunk likes you,'' she told Miranda.

''The hunk is trying to find out who robbed the store. Period.''

Suzanne rolled her eyes. ''I know what a man looks like when he's interested. He's definitely got it.''

''He was staring at you,'' Miranda felt compelled to point out.

''But he was listening to you.''

Miranda returned home to find chaos.

''Ms. Kirk, you want us to finish this driveway?'' Alvin Conroy, the foreman and owner, demanded.

''Of course—'' She wasn't given a chance to finish.

''The cops have been busting our chops most of the day. How're we supposed to do our jobs when the blues move in?''

''I don't—''

''You tell them we robbed you?''

''No—''

"Then get them off our backs."

Alvin "Rock" Conroy owned Rock-Hard Pavements. He was also the nephew of her dry cleaner. Neighborhood loyalties plus a desire to keep on the good side of the man who restored many of her treasures had prompted Miranda to hire Alvin to repave her driveway.

"Alvin—"

"Rock."

Alvin was two hundred and forty pounds of muscle in torn jeans and a cement-spattered T-shirt. His given name was a constant source of vexation, hence the nickname Rock.

"Rock," she tried again. "I'm sorry. I didn't know the police were going to question you and your crew. I'll make sure they don't bother you again." And she would, she vowed silently.

Mollified, Alvin nodded.

"I'm sorry," she apologized again. "It won't happen again."

When Tomás Dominguez, Juan's father, showed up an hour later, she had a pretty good idea what had happened.

"The police . . . they come . . . they think we stole from you."

The distress in his eyes tore at her heart. She did her best to reassure him that it was all a mistake and that she wanted his family to continue cleaning her store.

After visiting with the entire family and assuring them of her faith in them, she returned home, exhausted and sick at heart. The Dominguezes had endured so much in their homeland. The United States had been a new beginning, a place to relearn trust and hope.

With one fell swoop, MacKenzie Torrence had destroyed that.

Phones shrilled and mild curses cut through the air as she walked into the precinct station an hour later. The air-conditioning huffed ineffectually against the heat of an Indian summer. Her eyes watered at the smoke-filled air, underlaid by the gummy smell of pine disinfectant.

She'd been primed and ready, rehearsing her lines on the drive to the precinct. But as much as she'd been spoiling for a fight, the reality of the station house robbed her of breath. It had been years since she'd been inside a police station. The rush of memories stunned her. She braced herself against a wall and ordered herself to breathe.

A reminder that she was here to do a job steadied her, and she approached the first man she saw.

"I'm looking for Detective Torrence."

"Mac?" The man jerked a thumb toward an inner office. "He's holed up with the captain."

"I'll wait."

"I'm Mac's partner. Jake Shay. Maybe I can help you."

"It's private." Too late she realized the implication of her words.

She was shaking inside and out and folded her arms across her middle to try to control her anger. "I mean, I have to see Detective Torrence about a case."

"Sure. Have a seat." He gestured to a hard-backed chair.

She spent a moment absorbing the smells and noises of the squad room. Now that the initial shock was over, she could remember the good times as well. The occasional days when her father had taken her to work with him and showed her around. The hustle and bustle of men and women joking and working together. The feeling that her daddy was respected and looked up to. No, the memories weren't all bad. That thought braced her.

Mac gave a growl of disgust as he stalked back to his desk. He'd just been called on the carpet for mouthing off to a member of the city council.

When the blustering man appeared in the captain's office, demanding an apology, Mac had nearly lost his temper . . . and his job. Apologizing to the council member didn't do a thing to improve his disposition. Or his reputation.

"You're not a team player," the captain had said. Mac's scowl deepened. The men and women he worked with, respected, and liked, they were his team. He'd risked his life with them and for them and expected them to do the same.

Politicians. They wanted their cake and everyone else's too.

He plowed a hand through his hair and swallowed the taste of the stale coffee that he'd been obliged to sip in the process of making nice.

Finding Miranda waiting for him was a bright speck in an otherwise gray day. His smile slipped a notch when he took in the fiery expression in her eyes. The lady wasn't here to pay a social call, he thought with a wry twist of his lips, and congratulated himself on his deductive powers.

She stood. "Why did you do it?" she demanded before he even reached his desk.

Her voice was November-afternoon cold. The kind of cold that could slice right through a man. The kind of cold that told him to back off.

But he couldn't. He had a burglary to solve.

He didn't need this kind of grief. Not today. Not from her.

"Why don't you tell me what I did?" He met her

gaze, not even trying to hide the exhaustion he was sure was showing through.

"What gives you the right to question my friends, to scare the men working for me half to death?" she demanded.

Mac drew in a deep, slow breath, willing patience. Two hours' sleep over the last two days didn't make it any easier. He watched as she lifted her chin.

"Alvin didn't look particularly scared," Mac said.

He hadn't, she silently acknowledged. He'd been darn mad. But it wasn't Alvin she was concerned about. It was the Dominguezes.

She said as much and glared at him. "What'd you do, Detective? Pull out the rubber hoses?"

"Don't forget the bright lights and sodium Pentothal," he said, his own temper dangerously close to the surface. His jaw worked as tension clenched his teeth together. He struggled to adjust his mood. It wasn't her fault she'd caught him at a particularly bad time.

Her scowl said she didn't appreciate his sarcasm. "You've got nerve."

"What I got was an hour's sleep. That makes two, maybe three, in the last two days. Oh, don't forget the two extra cases the captain dropped on my desk. Add that to the ten or so that were already there and you've got yourself an even dozen."

He advanced toward her with a look that had her

unconsciously bracing herself. He stopped his march a few scant inches in front of her, the look on his face enough to cause her to want to retreat a few inches of her own. But she held her ground, head up, eyes level with his.

"Like it or not, lady, your shop was tossed. Somebody wants something you've got. I'm trying to stop them before they come back again. Next time, you might not be so lucky."

That had the effect of lifting her chin yet another notch.

Sweet heaven, she was beautiful. Mac had never denied that, but it had never taken hold of him in quite the same way it did now. She looked up at him, defiant and angry and totally desirable.

He gave in to temptation and pulled her to him.

For a moment, he forgot that he was supposed to be on the job. Forgot that he was investigating a robbery. Forgot everything but the woman he held in his arms. He lifted his head and tried to remember who and what he was.

She appeared equally shaken. Her breath came in sharp gasps that she couldn't hide.

He released her, watching as she struggled to compose herself. He was having a hard time doing that very thing.

His feelings were way out of line. He was a cop,

she a victim of a crime. He had no business thinking what he was thinking, feeling what he was feeling.

"It's ridiculous investigating them." Miranda fisted her hands on her hips and reined in her temper. For the first time, she noticed the lines fanning outward from the corners of his eyes. He looked infinitely weary.

That had the effect of deflating much of her anger. She knew he was only doing his job, but she couldn't let her friends be intimidated.

"Look, Miranda. It's time you started living in the real world. Chances are that whoever robbed you is someone you've met. Someone you know. Maybe even someone who works for you."

"You're way off base, Detective," she said, but her voice lacked its earlier fire.

"So you say. People who have nothing to hide don't get upset about being questioned by the police."

"The Dominguezes were so scared they could hardly tell me what happened," she said.

He frowned, silently acknowledging that the family had appeared frightened. He'd tried to be nonthreatening, even gentle, while questioning them. Apparently, he hadn't succeeded.

"I'm sorry about that," he said.

She gave him a long look. "I believe you are. But that doesn't change the fact that you scared them half to death."

"You think I get off terrifying people like that?"

"No. I don't." She sounded like she meant that. He didn't stop to analyze why the knowledge filled him with relief.

"Are you satisfied now that they had nothing to do with this?"

He didn't answer.

"You still think they might be involved?"

"I think it's a possibility."

Quicksilver anger flashed in her eyes, and she took a deep breath, obviously intending to tell him just what she thought of him.

He forestalled her by holding up a hand. "When I've got as few leads as I do now, I don't rule out anything—or anyone."

That had the effect of shooting gold into her chocolate-colored eyes.

"Does that include me?"

He thought of the honesty that shone in everything she did, everything she said. "No. It doesn't." His voice had turned unaccountably husky. It was time for a change of subject. "What about your assistant? Did I frighten her too?"

"Uh . . . Suzanne doesn't get rattled easily." Miranda studied the toes of her shoes. The truth was that Suzanne had enjoyed every bit of the questioning.

"He's a babe," she'd told Miranda after Mac had

interviewed her earlier that day. "A total babe. Why should I mind him asking me a couple of questions?"

Not for the first time Miranda thought about her odd friendship with Suzanne.

"You all right?" Mac asked. "You looked like you were a thousand miles away."

"Not quite that far. Just lay off my friends, okay?"

"As soon as I find out who tossed your store, I'll be out of your life. Fair enough?"

"Fair enough."

She wondered why she didn't feel better at the prospect. With sudden clarity, she knew. Under the layers of duty and suspicion, there was a man with strengths and vulnerabilities, a man she was coming dangerously close to liking.

She reminded herself that he was a cop. As far as she was concerned, that made him off-limits. There was no reason for her pulse to start galloping and her mouth to go dry just because he had the most expressive eyes she'd ever seen.

"Truce?" he asked.

"Truce."

For the barest of seconds, she could have sworn his gaze lingered on her lips, making her feel warm and syrupy all over. Then his gaze lifted, and she was left to wonder if she'd imagined those moments.

Chapter Three

The front door opened and the deliveryman walked in, carrying several packages. Out of the corner of her eye, she saw Sergeant Sanders tense.

He was trying, she conceded, as she signed the receipt and directed the deliveryman to take the boxes to the back room. As much as a man could appear unobtrusive in a woman's clothing store, he was doing his best as he sat in the corner, a folded newspaper propped over his legs.

A little balding, with an engaging smile, he looked as if he were waiting for his wife or girlfriend to come out of the dressing room so he could pass his opinion on the outfit she had selected.

Miranda smiled as she noticed several of the ladies

preen and primp as they pretended to study their reflections in the mirrors. She knew the sergeant was happily married. Even so, he sucked in his gut as the customers eyed him.

She turned away before he saw her smile, not wanting to embarrass him. He really was a dear. He didn't send off any of the disturbing signals Detective Torrence did.

Her smile vanished at that. MacKenzie Torrence was off-limits. Just because he was the most intriguing man she'd met in years didn't mean she was going to give in to the attraction that had been simmering between them for the last few days.

Cops had only one agenda: solving the case. That was what she needed from Mac. That was *all* she needed.

Then why was she having so much trouble convincing her heart of that?

Suzanne breezed in a half hour late. She gave Sanders a sunny smile before turning to Miranda. "Where's the hunk?" she whispered.

"Detective Torrence is busy. He's assigned Sergeant Sanders to keep an eye on things."

Mac had told her in confidence that Sanders would be moving from store to store, trying to identify anyone who didn't belong, anyone who lingered too long.

"Detective Torrence? He told me to call him Mac."

Suzanne smiled slyly. "He'd probably tell you the same thing if you were a little friendlier."

Miranda barely bit back a retort. Normally Suzanne's interest in anything in pants amused her. Now she was annoyed. "Don't you have some work to do?" she asked more sharply than she'd intended.

Hurt flashed in her friend's eyes before she turned away.

Miranda started after her and then stopped herself. How did she explain her bad temper to Suzanne when she didn't fully understand it herself? The answer came in an unsettling realization: she was jealous.

Mac wasn't the man for her, but she didn't want anyone else to have him either. Her dog-in-the-manger attitude shamed her. A silent lecture on the evils of jealousy did little to improve her mood.

She was about to apologize to Suzanne when Mac showed up. A leather bomber jacket stretched across broad shoulders. Jeans worn white at stress points emphasized the muscular length of his legs. Unaccountably nervous, she pulled a candy bar from her stash behind the counter, needing the rush of sugar and chocolate.

Mac had five open cases, a court appearance to make, and a mountain of paperwork cluttering his desk. Still, he found time to stop in at Buckles and Bows.

The need to see her had been a great deal stronger than the hunger that gnawed at his stomach, a result of skipping breakfast. It had been, he admitted, stronger than any need he'd ever experienced.

He told himself he needed to update Miranda about the case. The fact was that he didn't have anything to report. He simply wanted to see her again, though he didn't need the visit to recall what she looked like. Her face was imprinted on his memory—the shape of her chin, the texture of her skin, the curve of her cheek.

If he had a romantic streak, he might have thought in terms of poetry or music. Instead, he told himself he wanted only to make certain she was all right.

"Hi, Detective Hunk."

Suzanne's greeting raised a grin from him. The kid was cute in an offbeat way. But it was her boss who sent his blood pressure soaring. He felt like he'd been kicked in the gut as she smiled up at him.

She wore a silk dress that flowed around her legs as she walked, whispering with each movement. A wispy strip of lace cinched her narrow waist, a feminine bit of fluff that made her look good enough to eat.

Her scent was different today, something delicate and floral. He took a deep breath and identified the fragrance. Lily of the valley.

Funny. He'd always thought he'd fall for a tall

woman, one who matched him in height, not a slip of a girl a good foot shorter than his own six feet two.

It didn't help his disposition any when Sanders stared at her as if he were a starving man and she a seven-course dinner. One look from Mac and Sanders lowered his gaze, but not before Mac had caught the sergeant's grin.

Okay. His secret was out. He liked the lady. And he didn't want other men, even a friend, ogling her. Besides, Sanders was married with three kids.

He recognized his feelings as irrational. That didn't stop him from having them, though. Not by a long shot.

"I . . . uh . . ." Rational thought left him as she smiled up at him. His gaze fastened on the candy bar she held. "That stuff will kill you."

"I thought cops lived on junk food."

"Not this one."

"Don't tell me you're the yogurt and tofu type."

"Guilty as charged."

"I thoughts cops always ate doughnuts on the job." She couldn't help teasing him. He appeared almost embarrassed by the admission.

"You ought to try it," he said with a grimace directed at her candy bar.

"What do you mean?" she asked in a mock-affronted voice. "This contains the four basic food groups."

He lifted an eyebrow in inquiry.

''Sugar, fat, salt, and chocolate.''

The laughter in his eyes sparked a response deep within her, one completely out of proportion to the conversation. What had started as lighthearted banter had turned into something else. Something threatening to her well-being.

She wanted to step into his arms, to learn what it felt like to be held by him, to have his lips on hers, both demanding and tender. But there were reasons, she reminded herself, as she held back, good, strong reasons to resist him and the temptation he offered.

The man was fast becoming important to her. More important than a cop assigned to the case she was involved in.

She couldn't afford that. Deliberately, she took a step back and watched as his eyes narrowed.

''Something wrong?'' he asked.

''Nothing,'' she mumbled. ''I just remembered something I ought to be doing.''

''Something like keeping up that invisible wall you put up between us every time I get too close?''

The man was too perceptive by half. ''And if I were?''

''I'd wonder what you're afraid of.''

That had the effect of making her bristle. ''What I do is no concern of yours.''

''That's where you're wrong, honey. Very wrong.''

He gave her one of those turn-her-life-upside-down smiles.

She stared at him, bemused and wondering how he had managed to trip-hammer her heart with only a smile. Clearly, the man was a magician.

"Did you want to see me about something besides my poor eating habits, Detective?"

"Mac," he corrected automatically.

"Mac." Her soft voice made his matter-of-fact name sound like something special. "Did you have some news about the case?"

The case. Every time he got within a few feet of the lady, he forgot everything else. Even his job. The realization jolted him.

"Have dinner with me tonight." The words tumbled out before he had a chance to lead up to the invitation.

Miranda stared at him, clearly surprised.

He didn't blame her. After the lecture he'd given himself about keeping their relationship strictly professional, he'd surprised himself.

"Why?" she asked at last.

The invitation had been an impulsive one, prompted by something he didn't understand. But the need to spend time with her, to learn what made her laugh, what made her cry, was overriding common sense.

"I like you. I think you like me. We both have to eat. Why not do it together?"

"Sorry. I'm busy."

He recognized the excuse as the standard-issue one when a woman wasn't interested. But he'd have sworn she felt the same attraction for him that he did for her. He couldn't have mistaken the awareness that sparked between them the few times they'd been together.

His social life had taken a backseat to his job in the past few years, but he wasn't totally obtuse in recognizing the signals of interest between a man and a woman.

"Tomorrow night," he tried.

"I'm doing quarterly taxes."

That was a new one. "When *will* you be free?"

"Look, Mac. I appreciate what you're doing for me, trying to solve the case and all, but I'm just not interested."

"Why not?"

"Does every woman you meet fall at your feet?" she asked tartly.

"Not everyone," he said, the mischief in his eyes nearly drawing a smile from her.

She could have been tossing flowers at him, for all the reaction her rejection caused.

"Forget it, Detective. You're not my type."

"How do you figure?"

"Macho cops aren't my style."

"Maybe you'll make an exception."

She gave him a look designed to freeze him in his tracks.

"Sorry. I don't date cops."

He'd been so busy enjoying their banter and the sweet scent of her that the words failed to register at first. When they sank in, he gave her a quizzical look. "You're kidding. Right?" The humor in his eyes invited her to agree, to take back the words that had dimmed the brightness of the day.

"I'm sorry."

The amusement faded, to be replaced by a thoughtful frown. "You're serious, aren't you?"

"Look, Mac. I like you."

Was that regret in her voice? A ghost of a smile traced his lips. "That sounds like a brush-off."

"Not a brush-off. That would mean there was something between us. Think of it as thanks, but no thanks."

"You don't like cops?"

"I like cops just fine. My father was one." The annoyance that crossed her face told him she hadn't meant to say that.

"So why won't you go out with me?"

"What's the matter, Mac? Can't you take no for an answer?"

"I don't know. This is a first."

That drew a smile from her, as he'd intended.

"Nothing wrong with your ego, is there?" she asked.

"Not until recently." He reached for her hand and was encouraged when she didn't pull away. "If you like cops, then why won't you see me?"

"Personal policy."

"Then I'll have to change your mind. I always did like a challenge."

She drew in a sharp breath. The man's arrogance was unbelievable. She said as much, earning a smile from him.

"Back off, Detective."

Color bloomed on her cheeks. He'd annoyed her. Good. That was better than indifference. He was but a scant inch from her, and her breath brushed across his face. Sweet and warm, it came in short gasps that told him she wasn't as unaffected by him as she pretended to be.

"I'm a man first, a cop second."

"Sorry." She really was. "I can't separate the two."

"Try."

"No." The uncompromising tone of her voice had him raising his eyebrows.

"Care to tell me why?"

"It's private."

"Not when you tell me to get lost."

She let out a slow breath. "Let's just say I'm not

into waiting for the phone to ring or for you to show up because you were held up on a stakeout.''

''Is that what you think dating a cop is like?''

''I know what *living* with a cop is like.''

He took her hand. ''Maybe I can change your mind. Good thing I'm such a catch.''

She wouldn't smile. She wouldn't. In an effort to keep the smile she felt threatening from breaking through, she clamped her lips together. But her sense of humor got the best of her, and a laugh bubbled out, easing away the wrinkles of tension between them.

''See?''

''What I see is . . .''

Instinctively, she made to pull her hand away when he caught it, gently uncurling her bent fingers. One by one, he straightened them, kissing each fingertip in turn.

''We can start small,'' he said, appearing unaffected by the quickening of her pulse. Only the darkening of his eyes gave evidence to his churning feelings. ''You don't have to marry me right away. We can date for a while.'' A satisfied smile settled over his face as if he'd just reached an important decision.

It was difficult not to return the smile when he was looking at her with humor and—she stared into his eyes—loneliness.

''Please.'' She hated the pleading note in her voice. But she couldn't let this man into her life.

Mac stepped closer. Too close. So close that her shoulder brushed his chest and the curve of her cheek was only a scant inch from his mouth. Something sparked between them, a lightning arc of shimmering awareness.

She sucked in a breath, startled by his nearness. He was staring at her with eyes darkened to the color of old pewter. Though he made no move to touch her, she could feel him just the same. He was touching her as clearly as if he'd reached out and caressed her with those big hands.

Instinctively, she took a step back, but backed into the desk. Trapped, she looked up at him.

The heat in his gaze sent her pulse scattering, and she knew that he wanted to kiss her. She had never been so sure of anything in her life. And, heaven help her, she wanted him to kiss her, wanted it more than she'd ever wanted anything.

Kiss me, she wanted to shout, but the words caught in her throat.

What was she thinking? An involvement with a cop was the last thing she wanted, the last thing she needed. So why couldn't she tear her eyes away from his face as he lowered it to hers?

His mouth was but a whisper away. Another minute and she'd know what it felt like pressed against her own.

The shrilling of the phone shattered the moment.

She didn't know whether she was relieved or disappointed. A little bit of both, she decided as she picked up the receiver and then handed it to Mac. "It's for you."

"Yeah," she heard him say. "I understand. I'll get back to you."

Breathing space. The phone call had given them both breathing space, and she was determined to take advantage of it.

She had seconds to compose herself and hoped her face wasn't as red as it felt. "What's up?" she asked when he turned back to her.

"The lab boys managed to pick up a couple of partials that didn't belong to you. Or to me." He paused. "That's the good news."

"What's the bad?"

"They ran them and didn't find a match. Which means our perp either doesn't have a record or has never been printed."

"You said he must be a professional. You'd think a man like that would have been picked up sometime."

"Not if he's as good as I think he is."

"So we're back where we started."

"Just about." The discouragement in his voice echoed her own.

The almost-kiss was pushed aside. But not forgotten, she thought. She couldn't forget what had promised to be the most stirring kiss she'd ever experienced.

"I'll see you later," he said and let himself out.

She could only nod, not trusting her voice. When she turned around, it was to find Suzanne staring at her, a speculative gleam in her eyes.

"Has he asked you out yet?" Suzanne asked when Mac had left.

Miranda pretended an interest in the silk flower pinned to her suit. "He asked."

"And you said yes. Right?" her assistant prodded when Miranda remained silent.

"I told him I don't date cops."

"You told the most gorgeous man in the city, possibly the whole state, that you don't date cops. Why?" Suzanne's outrage rang in every word.

"You know why," Miranda said in a low voice.

"I know you have some crazy rule about dating cops. I didn't say anything before because the situation never came up. Now I'm saying it. You're crazy."

"It was a dinner invitation," Miranda said, weary of the conversation. "I turned him down. No big deal."

Suzanne gave her a long-suffering look. "I haven't seen you this interested in any man in months. Make that years. Maybe you shouldn't be so quick to write him off as a suitable candidate."

"Who said I was looking for 'suitable candidates'?'' Miranda demanded, hating the way her voice came out breathless instead of merely annoyed.

"I did." Suzanne's smug answer grated, but Miranda kept her expression neutral.

She didn't need this, she told herself. A cop who wouldn't leave her alone, a best friend who refused to mind her own business.

"Why don't you give him a chance?" Suzanne asked. "What's one date?"

Trouble. The word popped into her mind immediately. MacKenzie Torrence was trouble with a capital *T.*

She'd seen how having a cop in the family turned lives inside out. On occasion, it even took them. She wouldn't be a part of that. Never again.

At the precinct, Mac thought again about Miranda and her casual dismissal of him for no other reason than his job. The unfairness of it offended his sense of justice.

But it was more than that.

He wasn't accustomed to people challenging him. Maybe it came from being the oldest son in a large family. Maybe it came from being a cop. Maybe it came from an overactive ego, just as Miranda had accused him of. He killed the smile touching his lips before it was fully born.

He didn't chase women. He particularly didn't chase a woman who said flat out that she wasn't interested. Or one who was sending out mixed signals. He didn't play games, didn't believe in them. If he was attracted to a woman, he let her know it.

Since Miranda had told him thanks but no thanks, he should have shrugged off his attraction and moved on. The thing was, he couldn't.

It had been over a week since he'd asked her to have dinner with him. He'd be darned if he was going to pick up the phone and call her. He'd asked her out; she'd refused. End of story.

He was going to put Miranda Kirk out of his mind and focus solely on solving the case. He issued a heavy sigh. He had a feeling both were easier said than done.

The lady had a thing about cops. Well, that wasn't unusual. His job had cost him more than one relationship in the past. But this time was different. *She* was different.

He sighed a bit as he recalled the confrontation they'd had—he couldn't think of it as anything else. He hadn't gotten anywhere with her. Not a fraction of an inch. She'd put up the barriers at the mention of something more between them and hadn't lowered them.

Every argument he'd laid out for keeping his distance from her still existed. Nothing had changed, yet he couldn't stop thinking about her.

He tried to decipher the signals she gave off, first warm, then cool, then indifferent. Tried and failed.

Miranda was an enigma. Warm and open at times, reserved and closed at others. He'd earned his detective's badge by studying the subtle signs by which people revealed—and concealed—themselves. Surely one small woman could offer no great challenge to a skill honed by fifteen years on the force.

But she did.

So what was bothering him? It was the way she made him feel—as though he needed to protect her, take care of her, in ways that had nothing to do with his being a cop. And everything to do with his being a man.

Mac wasn't accustomed to needing. He didn't much care for the sensation. But that didn't stop him from thinking about Miranda. He wondered how she'd react if she knew how much time he spent doing just that. Thinking about her.

Probably tell him where to get off, he thought with a wry smile.

The lady had made it plain that she didn't date cops. Well, that was all right. He wasn't looking for a relationship, didn't need one. The refrain was beginning to wear old. The fact was, he wanted to be with her.

"We're not finished yet, lady," Mac muttered under his breath, not to be put off by a woman who intrigued him.

When his feelings spilled over into his work, he knew he was in trouble. He snapped at Jake Shay, his partner and friend, when Jake started in on him about Miranda. "Sanders says you got a thing for the pretty lady."

Mac gave a low growl. "Maybe Sanders oughta mind his own business."

"That go for me too?" Jake asked in an even voice.

Mac realized he was out of line. "Sorry."

Jake shook his head, looking sorrowful. "You got it bad, buddy."

Mac gave his friend a good-natured poke in the arm. "Thanks. Why don't you go brighten someone else's day?"

"You need me."

"That'll be the day," Mac muttered.

"Trust those instincts you're always bragging about. Give yourself and Miranda a chance."

Mac gave his friend a wry smile. "I don't see you rushing to the altar."

"If I found a woman like Miranda, I just might." His partner grinned slyly. "If you're not interested, maybe I'll try my luck."

Hot jealousy surged through Mac at the idea of some other man going after Miranda. Even his best friend. Especially his best friend. "Leave her alone."

Jake held up his hands in surrender. "Whatever you say, partner."

Mac caught the grin edging his friend's lips. He'd been had. "You're real funny."

Jay's smile was all innocence. "I try."

Chapter Four

Mac didn't like what he was thinking, what he was feeling. He prayed he was wrong. When he found that Juan Dominguez had a juvenile record, he feared Miranda had lied to him.

He showed up at her house unannounced.

"I didn't know you were coming." For an unguarded moment, her eyes lit with something like pleasure.

"Neither did I."

"Something's happened," she said slowly.

"Yeah. You could say that."

The pleasure faded to be replaced with a frown as she registered the expression in his eyes. "What's wrong?" She looked up at him, her eyes wide and vulnerable. "What is it?" she persisted when he remained silent.

He looked about, needing something to divert his attention. "What's that?" He pointed to what looked like a lump at the end of the sofa.

"That's Norman."

"Norman? As in Schwarzkopf?"

"As in *City Slickers.*" At his blank look, she explained, "You know, the little calf in the movie."

"He's a dog."

"Very observant, Detective."

Norman lumbered down from the sofa and wandered over to Mac, sniffed once, twice, then settled at his feet.

"Some watchdog," Mac said.

"He's just friendly."

Mac bent to pet Norman, scratching him behind the ears. The dog made a low growling noise that was meant to be threatening, Mac supposed. It came out like a whine.

"He's hungry," she said.

From the look of Norman, he hadn't missed many meals, Mac thought. A glance at Miranda's face as she petted the dog and he kept the thought to himself. Obviously, she was crazy about the dog.

Jealousy, hot and unreasonable, rose up within him. Jealous over a dog. He was losing it. Big time.

He took her elbow, steering her toward the door. "We have to talk."

"Okay."

"Not here." He didn't want to question her in her home. It was too personal, too intimate. "There's a diner not far from here."

"McGuilicutty's," she said, nodding. "I'll get my coat." She murmured something to Norman, then walked to the hall closet and came back with a fleecy jacket. "I'm ready."

Was that guilt he saw in her eyes? Or something else?

The silence thickened until it filled the car. Mac's jaw was set so tightly she could practically feel the grinding of his teeth.

Neither spoke until they were seated inside the comfortably heated diner.

Miranda ordered hot chocolate, hoping the warm, sweet liquid would restore her flagging energy. Mac ordered coffee, black. It suited his mood, she thought uncharitably.

Ever since he'd appeared at her door, his face had resembled a thundercloud, his craggy brows drawn together in a fierce scowl. A muscle in his jaw ticked. She'd been loath to break in on his self-imposed silence, but enough was enough. She felt her temper begin to unravel, strand by strand.

The waitress had appeared with their drinks, and

Miranda gratefully curled her cold fingers around the mug, letting its warmth seep through her skin. She took a cautious sip, then another, all the while watching Mac.

He downed his coffee in one long gulp, causing her to wince in sympathy. The steam rising from his cup told her the coffee was hot enough to scald his tongue. He didn't appear affected by it, though. He continued to glower at everyone and everything, his angry gaze enough to keep the approaching waitress from offering refills.

"Okay," she said. "Let's have it. What's got you so riled up?"

"Juan Dominguez has a record." He gave her a moment to digest that. "It started out small enough. Shoplifting, joyriding. Then he joined a gang and the ante went up. The Blades." The Blades were the most notorious juvenile gang in Denver.

She nodded slowly. "I know."

"And you didn't see fit to tell me."

She'd lied to him. Looked at him with those guileless brown eyes and lied to him. He'd known, but he'd hoped. How he'd hoped. Her honesty was one of the things he liked best about her. She could no more hide her feelings than she could lie. Or so he thought. Disappointment sliced through him. He shook it off. He had a job to do, a job that didn't allow for personal feelings.

"Why didn't you tell me?"

"It didn't seem important."

"Didn't seem important?" Anger brushed his voice, a cold, hard anger that had her flinching. He couldn't regret it. She'd jeopardized the case, her own safety, with her silence.

She held her ground. "The Dominguezes would never hurt me. And Juan's cleaned up his act."

"The Blades aren't famous for letting their members go. How'd he get out?"

"Check out the scars on his arms."

She didn't say anything more. She didn't need to. If what she said was true, the gang had exacted retribution on Juan. But that didn't change what she'd done.

"You held back information that could break this case." He'd known her loyalty to her friends ran deep. But at what risk? Didn't she realize her life could be in danger?

"I've been doing some more checking," he said. "Juan and his family worked at three out of five of the stores that have been hit."

"That doesn't prove anything."

By itself, it didn't. Added to Juan's involvement with a gang, it could.

He stared at Miranda, unable to tear his gaze away. She retained a freshness and faith in people that he'd lost somewhere along the way. He only hoped that faith hadn't been misplaced.

"You're wrong about him," she said in that same quiet voice.

Maybe he was. That didn't change things. She hadn't trusted him enough to tell him about Juan. What else hadn't she told him? What else had she lied about, if only by omission?

Her honesty was one of the things that had first attracted him to her. That, he admitted, and a first-class set of legs.

"I have to talk with him."

Her chin came up, a defiant gesture that grated along his already tense nerves. "Why can't you take my word that he isn't involved?"

"Why can't you trust me?" There was an ice-and-steel edge to his voice this time. Underlying it, though, was pain. That annoyed him.

They glared at each other, a silent battle of wills.

"Do you know where Juan is now?" he asked at last.

She looked like she was about to refuse. "The Cardware store, down the street from my shop. He and his parents clean it every Friday night."

"Thanks."

He supposed her scowl was her answer. It couldn't be helped. He started to stand up when her voice stopped him.

"Mac."

"What?

"It won't make any difference if you question him tonight or tomorrow, will it?"

"No." He bit out the word.

"Will you do something for me?" She didn't wait for his answer. "Give yourself time. Right now you're angry at me." She didn't say anything more. She didn't have to. The implication was clear.

"And you think I'll let that influence my judgment when it comes to Juan?"

"I think it's possible," she said carefully.

Great. Just great. First she'd lied to him. Then she questioned his professional integrity. He'd never harmed a witness or prisoner in his care. He wasn't about to start now. The lady knew how to twist the knife.

"Have him at your place tomorrow. You can stay with him if you're so afraid of what I'll do." Something in her eyes compelled him to add, "I'm sorry."

"So am I."

She didn't back down and she didn't back off. Reluctant admiration sparked through him even as irritation kicked through him at her head-in-the-sand attitude.

Miranda believed in loyalty and being there for her friends. The Dominguez family didn't know how lucky they were. Maybe they did at that, he thought, remembering the concern in their eyes when he'd told them about the break-in at Miranda's store.

He couldn't bring himself to believe that they were involved. But Juan's record couldn't be ignored. He had to investigate the boy. To do less would be unprofessional at best, life threatening at worst.

But his heart wasn't in it. Like it or not, Miranda's faith in the boy had influenced his judgment.

"I'll take you home," he said.

Hours later, Mac gave up the battle to sleep.

It had been years since he'd been so intrigued by a woman, and longer still since he'd felt about one a fraction of what he did for Miranda.

Even the disappointment he'd experienced tonight failed to dilute that interest.

She had more sides than a multifaceted diamond. Warm and giving one moment, cool and distant the next. She was at once exasperating and exciting, maddening and mysterious, and totally enchanting. She deliberately kept him at arm's length, as if scared of letting him get too close. That much was clear. Just how deep it went, though, he wasn't sure.

The idea that Miranda might be frightened caused him to pause. The more he thought about it, the more convinced he became that he was right. A mystery, he thought. He never could resist one, needing to pick it apart, layer by layer, until he found the heart of it.

It didn't excuse the on-and-off signals she sent out, but it went a long way toward explaining them. And as much as she pretended otherwise, he knew she wasn't indifferent toward him.

He couldn't mistake the tension that singed the air whenever they were together. He knew she had to be aware of the electricity between them as well. He also knew she was fighting it.

He didn't know why, but he was determined to find out.

Maybe if he found a way to storm all those defenses she'd erected, he might find the real Miranda Kirk. The glimpses he'd managed to get so far were enough to convince him the result would be more than worth the effort.

He'd bide his time. If he moved too fast, he risked scaring her off. On the other hand, if he kept his feelings to himself forever . . . well, faint heart never won fair lady.

Only in this case, the fair lady wanted nothing to do with him.

Miranda pushed the curtains aside and sighed. A drizzly rain darkened the morning . . . and her mood. She refused to attribute it to her fight with Mac.

She knew she'd disappointed him, and her conscience smarted because of it. She'd hurt him. She hadn't meant to, hadn't wanted to, but that didn't change what she'd done.

Maybe she'd been wrong in keeping Juan's past from Mac. At the time, she'd thought only to protect a friend, to shield him from questioning that was certain to be painful. Now she wasn't so certain.

Had it been but one more roadblock in her relationship with Mac? Had she secretly hoped he'd find out and turn on her in anger, severing whatever was between them?

The idea repelled her. Still, she wondered. She was attracted to him. That much was a given. But attraction didn't have to be acted on.

By the time Mac showed up at her store, she was ready.

Miranda made the introductions, her voice betraying her anxiety. He wished he could skip this. But he had a job to do. And right now that job meant questioning someone she cared about.

When she turned to him, the unhappiness in her eyes stirred his protective instincts. He had a crazy impulse to wrap his arms around her and promise her that everything was going to be all right. Trouble was, he couldn't promise her anything.

Her gaze settled on Juan. The warmth of the smile she gave the boy was a punch to the gut. Mac took a deep breath. He'd never seen her smile so unguardedly before. Certainly, she'd never favored *him* with such warmth.

The boy was only of medium height, but he had the wiry strength of youth. A slight case of acne dotted his cheeks and chin, but he was otherwise good looking, with an engaging smile and intelligent eyes. He was at that gangly, in-between stage, rubbing uncomfortably against the edges of adulthood.

Juan had a confused look in his eyes now, as though he thought he should play the part of a man but the boy kept getting in the way.

"Juan, Detective Torrence wants to ask you some questions."

The boy's smile faded, but he didn't look away. "Sir."

Mac chalked up a point in Juan's favor. "I hear you've had some trouble in the past."

Juan nodded.

"You were mixed up with a gang."

Another nod.

"The Blades have a bad rep." That was putting it mildly. The Blades were the most notorious gang in Denver, with initiation rites that made even the most hardened cops blanch.

"I don't hang with them no more." Juan's voice held a trace of defiance. But underlying it was fear.

Mac saw Miranda's frown and guessed she was surprised by Juan's street talk. Mac had done some checking at Juan's school and knew he had a good record there, had even made the honor roll the last semester.

"Mind telling me where you were last Tuesday night?"

Juan's eyes darted from Miranda to Mac and then back to Miranda. "I don't remember."

"Try."

"Juan, please." Miranda laid a hand on his shoulder. "We want to help you."

The boy gave her a skeptical look. "Police don't help no one."

The look Miranda directed at Mac was warm and wary at the same time. "Detective Torrence isn't like that."

"Yeah?" Juan all but sneered the word.

Mac wasn't surprised by Juan's cynicism. He'd seen it frequently enough. Beneath the boy's tough-guy attitude, though, he sensed fear. He couldn't let that stop him from doing his job, though.

"You want to tell me where you were? We can do it here. Or downtown."

"I was at choir," Juan muttered.

Now it was Mac's turn to be skeptical. "Choir?"

Juan shifted from foot to foot. "We practice every Tuesday night."

"Who's we?"

"A class at church. The choir director there said I

had a gift.'' Juan's face reddened, but he went on doggedly. ''That maybe I could even get a scholarship. She's gonna help me.'' Juan turned to Miranda, his eyes desperate. ''That's all my parents can talk about—me going to college. I can't let 'em know. Not yet. In case things don't work out.'' His color deepened. ''And the guys at school . . . they'd never let me live it down if they found out I liked *singing.*''

Miranda looked at Mac. ''We'll keep your secret,'' she promised.

''I'll have to check it out,'' Mac warned, but he was pretty sure the boy was telling the truth. That flush was too genuine to be faked. ''Juan, thank you.''

For the first time since the questioning had begun, Juan smiled. ''I wouldn't do anything to hurt Ms. Kirk. She's been real good to my folks and me.''

Miranda curled a hand around his shoulder. ''Good luck on the scholarship. I'm rooting for you. If I can do anything, write a letter or something, let me know.''

''I know you are, ma'am. And thanks.'' He ducked his head, his cheeks brighter than ever. ''Can I go now?''

''Yeah,'' Mac said.

''Satisfied?'' Miranda asked when Juan had gone.

''I still have to check out his story,'' he repeated. ''But I don't think he had anything to do with it.''

Which left him with nothing. Still, he was relieved, for her sake, that Juan was clean.

"Back to square one?" she asked.

" 'Fraid so."

"Dad always said crimes were a puzzle. You had to make the pieces fit."

It was the first time she'd mentioned her father other than to say he'd been a cop. Intrigued, he wanted to ask why she was so opposed to dating cops when her father had been one. Impulse tumbled the question out before he could talk himself out of it.

She looked as if she'd been poleaxed.

"I'm sorry," he said. "I had no right asking."

Her eyes were bleak. "Dad died eighteen years ago."

He watched as she struggled with the emotions threatening to overwhelm her. Seconds bled into minutes, and he wondered if she'd tell him the rest.

"Dad was by-the-book all the way, an old-fashioned beat cop. But he always said a heart was a cop's best friend, that it would tell him what to do when he wasn't sure. He knew the names of all the kids on his street."

"He sounds like a remarkable man."

"He was." She stared into space, remembering. "He kept most of that part of his life from my mother and me, but he let us know that there was a right way and a wrong way to do things. It eventually got him killed. That and a misplaced devotion to duty.''

Now it was his turn to feel like he'd been hit in the solar plexus. He knew Miranda had mixed feelings about her father, but he hadn't realized the extent to which she'd blamed his work for his death.

''Most jobs have risks,'' he said carefully.

''Most jobs don't involve some drug-crazed kid waving a gun at you.''

''Is that how he died?''

She nodded. ''He wasn't even on duty that night. Mom was out of town, visiting relatives. Dad and I had rented *Casablanca* and decided we needed a snack while we were watching it, so we stopped at a convenience store to pick up some ice cream. A couple of kids were there. I didn't pay much attention. Then one of them pulled a gun and told the girl behind the cash register to empty it.

''Dad pushed me to the ground. He wounded one of the boys, but the other . . . the second one shot him.'' Her voice was tear-husky, but her eyes were dry. ''The store owner called nine-one-one, but it was too late. Dad died in my arms.''

The naked vulnerability in her eyes struck him like a physical blow as he took in what she'd just told him.

She'd seen her own father gunned down, held him while he lay dying. He wanted to hold her, to take away her pain. And he knew it was impossible. He lifted a finger to her cheek to wipe away the first tear, and when he did, her back straightened and she pulled away.

His heart ached for the child she'd been. He wanted to go back in time and find that small girl, to make everything right in her life. But all he could do was reach out to the woman.

He did that now, wrapping her in his arms and holding her to him, trying to absorb her pain. This time she didn't resist. They stayed locked together for long minutes. When she pulled away, he let her go.

Reluctantly.

"You loved him very much."

"I loved him. I hated what he did. I tried to make sense of what happened. But nothing ever did," she whispered, and he knew she had dropped into the past once again.

He'd persuaded himself that he could talk her out of her dislike of cops. He'd been fooling himself, he realized.

"Your father sounds like a good man."

"He was. It took me a long time to forgive him for leaving us."

He understood the feeling. He'd seen grief channeled into anger before. Anger was easier to deal with; it protected those left behind from acknowledging their grief. He also knew it didn't work. It sounded like Miranda had discovered that for herself.

Their gazes connected, and it came to Mac that he had never felt so close to anyone in his life. Never had anyone shared with him something that was so profound, so personal. More moved than he could ever remember being, he reached out to brush the hair from her face.

"Thank you," he said, his voice scarcely more than a croak. "For telling me."

"You had a right to know."

That gave him pause. "A right?"

"To understand why I can't . . ."

He understood now. "Why you can't become involved with a cop."

She nodded.

He dropped his hand. "I won't insult you by saying I know how you feel. But I have lost a partner. And I know you don't get over something like that. You learn to live with it, but you don't get over it."

"Then you understand?"

It was his turn to nod.

"Thank you."

"That doesn't mean I agree."

"You just said—"

"I said I understood. That's a long way from agreeing."

She turned away. He wanted to reach out to her, to bring her back from whatever darkness had drawn her into its abyss. But he kept silent, knowing she'd reject any comfort right now.

So he did the only thing he could.

It surprised her, the gentleness of his touch as he brushed his knuckles over her jaw. He was a man a woman could lean on, depend on when times were tough. For a heart-shattering moment, she was tempted to do just that. To lay her head on his shoulder, close her eyes, and let him comfort her, especially now as the past prowled through her, ready to pounce and rip into her.

The moment passed and she gave a silent sigh, relief warring with regret.

"Can I lock up?" Suzanne asked.

Miranda glanced around and saw that everyone had gone but the two of them. No doubt Suzanne was anxious to get home and prepare for a date. It had been a hectic day, with a constant stream of customers.

"Go on. I'll do it," Miranda said. "Hey," she called as Suzanne started toward the back room to collect her purse and coat. "Thanks. There'll be a bonus in your paycheck."

"No sweat," her assistant said.

Mac showed up then. He flashed a smile at Suzanne, but his attention was for Miranda. "I came to see you home."

"That's not necessary—"

"I think it is."

"He's a keeper," Suzanne told Miranda. With a sassy toss of her head, she was gone.

Miranda could feel the heat inch up her neck and onto her face. Someday Suzanne was going to go too far. She saw the world as one big date and wanted everyone matched up. If she'd lived in the time of Noah, she'd probably have paired off a grizzly bear and a kitten.

"She . . . uh . . . I'd better . . ."

Mac only grinned, further flustering her.

She glanced at the near-empty racks and shelves. Far from discouraging business, the publicity about the burglary had brought out more customers than ever. She and Suzanne had been working hard. "People bought everything in sight." She emptied the cash register, a little staggered by the day's total. "I need to take it to the night deposit at the bank."

Mac held her coat for her, letting his hands slide down her shoulders as she shrugged into it. A frisson of pleasure followed the trail of his hands.

She locked the door, then dropped the keys in her pocket. With Mac to accompany her, she decided to walk to the bank, a neighborhood branch that had opened in the last year. With a recommendation from her, the Dominguez family had secured the job of after-hours cleaning.

The air was cool, a soft breeze that caught her hair

in its wake. She pulled the barrettes out and let the curls blow free. She clutched the deposit bag under her arm, intensely aware of the man beside her.

He was watching her, a small smile tugging at his lips. ''You look good that way.''

Somehow, during their walk to the bank, he'd moved close. Uncomfortably close. Because of his height, she was forced to tilt her head back to meet his gaze. The encroaching darkness and accompanying shadows concealed his expression except for the glint in his gray eyes.

''You like the windblown look?''

''I like *you*. Gotta problem with that?''

''No.'' Her voice lacked conviction.

''Sure you do. We'll work on it.'' The husky note in his voice, as soft and deep as black velvet, shimmied down her spine.

She was grateful for the darkness, which concealed the color that crept up her cheeks. Mac had a way of throwing her off balance and keeping her there. A few words from him and she was blushing like a schoolgirl.

She had the uneasy feeling he was remembering that almost-kiss of a week ago. Every time she met his gaze for more than a moment, she was reminded of it.

She made the deposit, experiencing a quiet elation at the amount she filled in on the bank slip. This would go a long way to help pay off the loan she'd taken out to start up Buckles and Bows. Exhilarating though it had been, the day had caught up with her, and a yawn escaped.

''Come on,'' Mac said, taking her arm. ''You're asleep on your feet.''

She *was* tired, her muscles weeping with fatigue. But it was a heady exhaustion, the kind born of a satisfying day's work. They made the short trip back to her store and picked up her car. Mac insisted upon following her home.

''Thanks for seeing me home,'' she said outside her house.

''I've tried to pretend this isn't happening,'' he said. ''But I look at you and I can't think of anything else.''

He caught her hand in his and pulled her to him. She moved away when she felt her toes bump into his. For every step she took, though, he took one, guiding her backward until she was backed up against the wall.

Literally and figuratively.

Neither spoke. The slow ticking of the clock echoed her own heartbeat. Her pulse fluttered as his breath spilled over her collarbone. He slid his palms up her arms until he cradled her face in his hands. Instinctively, her hands went to his waist. She felt him stiffen at her touch.

Finally she could stand the silence no longer. ''Mac—''

He reached out to place a hand over her mouth, but

she turned her head just then. Instead of silencing her, he caught his fingers in her hair.

Her gaze flew to his while he painstakingly untangled his fingers. She stared at him for a second longer, before she tried again.

She wasn't allowed to finish this time either as his mouth covered hers. Her face captured between his hands, she could feel his warm breath against her skin, smell the minty scent of it.

It was hardly a kiss, more a brushing of lips against lips, the contact so brief as to be practically nonexistent. For a moment, she wondered if she'd imagined the whole thing. But the effect on her confirmed its reality. Her breathing had turned shallow, her palms hot. A searing awareness flashed through her as she realized that she wanted him to kiss her again.

The kiss was like nothing she'd experienced before. There was only sensation upon sensation. Firm lips with gentle pressure. Strong hands with a tender touch. And she liked it.

Heaven help her, she liked it.

She pulled back. "I didn't know. . . ."

"Didn't know what?"

"That it could be like this."

"Neither did I."

Miranda eased into wakefulness slowly. She'd had the night to settle her feelings, but they'd refused her efforts to arrange them in an orderly fashion.

Glancing out the window, she saw that night had given way to the bright light of day. The sun cast a pink glow over the cobblestone clouds that drifted through the sky.

She hadn't been able to get Mac out of her mind. She'd spent most of the night thinking of him, remembering the kiss they'd shared and, more telling, her response to it.

It had been exhaustion, she decided, that had prompted her reaction. Mac had sought to comfort her and she . . . well, she had responded to that comfort. Nothing more.

Her reaction to Mac couldn't be trusted. The smart thing to do would be to forget that those few minutes of intimacy had ever happened.

She spent the morning trying to convince herself of that. By the time she opened the doors of Buckles and Bows, she thought she'd succeeded.

Suzanne's arrival, only twenty minutes late, destroyed her hard-won composure. "How'd the date go?" she asked without preamble.

"It wasn't a date. Mac simply walked me to the bank and then followed me home."

"Fine. It wasn't a date. So how'd it go?" Eyes narrowed, Suzanne took a long look at her boss. "He kissed you, didn't he?"

"What makes you think that?" Miranda straightened a tray of jewelry.

"You did that yesterday," her assistant reminded her. "You look different. You're practically glowing." Suzanne gave her a knowing smile.

Why was she being so evasive? Miranda wondered. In the three years that Suzanne had worked for her, they'd never kept secrets from each other.

"Mac took me home, and then he kissed me." It was a bald account of the facts, and she put her hands to her cheeks, appalled that she had blurted it out that way.

"You're blushing."

"It was just a kiss. Nothing happened." The lie nearly caught in her throat. The memory of the kiss alone was enough to heat her cheeks and quicken her breathing.

"Nothing?"

"Nothing," Miranda repeated firmly.

"How was it?"

Wonderful. "It was okay." She felt her cheeks flush with heat. Again. Something flared directly under her heart, quickly banked.

"Maybe I'll ask the man himself."

The door opened then, and Mac walked in, letting in a gust of wind. The air left her lungs in a *whoosh* in that same moment. She gripped the counter and stared up at him.

"Hi." Her voice sounded much too breathless, and she swallowed, intending to try again.

Apparently Mac didn't sense anything wrong, for he gave her a half smile that had her wondering what would happen if he turned it on full force.

Suzanne smiled her Cheshire-cat smile. "I'll just let you two . . . discuss the case."

"Thanks." Mac waited until she had left the room before giving in to the impulse to draw Miranda into his arms.

He'd told himself it was simply concern for her that prompted his visit. She'd seemed disoriented, upset after the kiss last night. The truth was he couldn't stay away. Though he still hadn't convinced her to go out with him, he sensed a weakening in the barriers she'd put up between them.

"I had to see you." He'd spoken no more than the truth. "Just like I have to do this." He lowered his head and slanted his lips over hers.

The kiss, intended to pleasure them both, escalated into something else entirely. Lips touched, tested, then tasted. Hers were softly parted, sweetly yielding, and utterly tempting.

She appeared equally as shaken. "You . . . me . . ."

"Yeah," he said. "You and me."

"When the case is over, we can get on with our life."

Our life. It was probably no more than a slip of the tongue. Surely, Miranda couldn't be thinking along those lines.

Mac was, though. It came to him like a flash of divine revelation.

With Miranda, he had started thinking about white shutters and red brick, a couple of bikes in the yard, a pair of roller skates on the front step. The images teased his mind. Overriding all of them, though, was the thought of Miranda in his arms. He wanted to go to bed with her at night and wake up with her in the morning. He wanted to share the good times as well as the bad.

He wanted it all.

Chapter Five

The night was steamy after a thundershower. Even the buildings seemed to be sweating, the streets hissing from the recent rain. Denver's Colfax Avenue buzzed with the sounds of nightlife. Graffiti-scrawled walls, vacant lots littered with bottles and cans and heaven knew what else, people huddled in doorways sending furtive glances his way—the area was definitely the seamier side of the city.

Like the neighborhood, the bar where he was to meet his snitch had seen better days.

An oldie but goodie blared from the aging jukebox, its innocent lyrics about a woman wronged no match for the escalating din from the bar's patrons. Smoke, cigarette and something else, hung over the room in a stinging haze.

All in all, it was a dive, Mac thought. A seedy place where some men went to lose themselves and others, like him, to find something. Information was a commodity like any other. His wouldn't be found on the information superhighway, though.

No, Mac had sources of his own. Sources that didn't include computers and the Internet. Not that he disdained those tools. A man'd be a fool not to use whatever netted him what he needed.

Tonight he needed the dish on street news and so he was here, looking for a source that wouldn't know the Web from a spider's lair.

Sammy "the Wart" Warton was a snitch. Mac spotted him propped against the bar, a small man who blended in with the seedy surroundings. With oily black hair slicked back from a pimply forehead and eyes that darted everywhere but straight ahead, he shifted from one foot to the other, making Mac think of a nervous stork.

Sammy smelled of old beer and unwashed clothes. He had one redeeming quality: he had the ear. The ear was what made him a veritable warehouse of information. Sammy didn't know the Internet from the Interstate, but he had a network system to rival any more sophisticated one. When you needed certain kinds of intelligence, Sammy was your man.

''Another for my friend,'' Mac said, pushing a couple of bills to the bartender.

Sammy looked up, his small eyes narrowed in speculation. ''Hey, Mac.''

When the drink arrived, Sammy tapped his fingers against the frosty glass for a moment before tipping it up and swallowing the beer in one gulp. He coughed, then sucked in air through yellowed teeth. A gold crown winked in the back of his mouth, a surprising bit of glitter in an otherwise remarkably drab man.

Protective coloring, Mac thought, allowing Sammy to slip in and out of the many places he called home. Men like Sammy didn't have addresses. They had holes that they pulled in after them when they needed to disappear for a while.

Mac gave Sammy enough time to order another drink. The bartender raised his brow at Mac, who nodded.

''What do you know about a high-tech burglar who can bypass any alarm?''

Sammy took a swallow. ''This important?''

Mac bit back a sharp retort. ''Yeah. It's important.''

''What's it worth to you?''

Mac flashed a couple of twenties.

''That'll do for starts,'' Sammy said, starting to pocket the bills.

Smoothly, Mac drew the money back, ignoring

Sammy's wounded look. "First you talk; then I pay. Maybe."

Sammy looked hurt, then shrugged philosophically. "High tech, you say?"

"The best. Slips in and out of places without a trace."

"What's he after?"

"The usual. Jewelry. Anything easily fenced."

"You make it hard on a man," Sammy said in a whiny voice as his nostrils twitched.

"I came to the best," Mac said, stroking Sammy's already inflated ego.

Sammy preened. "You came to the right place." He scratched his bearded chin. "There's been some talk about a guy who uses a bunch of gadgets." He spoke with the disdain of a man who relied upon the traditional methods of crime and had no use for those who needed special devices.

A table tipped over in the far corner with the sound of breaking glass and loud, belligerent voices. Out of the corner of his eye, Mac saw the bartender glance nervously at the six-foot mirror hanging behind the bar.

Sammy ordered another beer, drained it faster than the first, then closed his fingers around the empty glass. "I can keep my eyes and ears open. For a price."

Mac produced the money once again and watched as Sammy pocketed it.

"Money's fine," Sammy said in that same whiny voice. "But this kind of work is going to cost you extra."

"What do you want?"

"Put in a good word with my parole officer. Guy's hassling me all the time."

"You keep your nose clean and I'll do what I can."

Mac was still thinking about Sammy as he booted up his computer at work. At first he'd had no use for computers and all the fancy programs that went with them. His father had been a beat cop, a cop's cop, and Mac saw himself as the same, even after he'd made detective.

In recent years, though, he'd started to appreciate the role computers played in law enforcement. New software helped solve any number of cases now—predicting moves, drawing up psychological as well as technical profiles, matching suspects to MOs.

That didn't mean good old-fashioned police work was outdated. Snitches, stakeouts, and wading through reams of paperwork would always be the backbone of breaking a case. But he wasn't above using whatever tools he had.

He entered what they knew about the perp, method of entry, type of items stolen, technical expertise. He sat back, studied the screen, and frowned. There was precious little.

He exited the computer and prayed Sammy came up with more than he had.

With a bag and paper-cup holder balanced in his arms, Mac rapped on Miranda's door. He'd decided to appeal to her appetite. He'd already discovered the lady had a love of sweets.

When she opened the door, he nearly dropped the bag. In a long satin robe that evoked pictures of the 1940s, she looked softly feminine and totally tempting.

"Since you won't have dinner with me, I thought we'd try breakfast." He didn't give her a chance to refuse but pressed a Styrofoam cup of coffee into her hands. "Decaf."

She made a face but accepted it. "Not bad," she said after a tentative swallow. "Is this part of your healthy lifestyle?"

"Uh-uh. It's takeout from the burger joint around the corner. They were out of the good stuff."

Her smile looked genuine now. "Good. I could never have a meaningful relationship with someone who actually likes this stuff."

A chagrined expression crossed her face, and he knew she regretted her choice of words. He wasn't going to press her on it, though. But a small glow of hope settled over his heart just the same.

She sat down at the table, wrapping her hands around the cup. It warmed her, but no more than the look in Mac's eyes as they rested on her. He pushed a plate of bagels and donuts toward her.

Companionably, they shared breakfast.

"Thanks."

Before she could stand up, he was there, offering her a hand.

Miranda took his hand. They were too close again. And she was too aware of him, of the intensity that shimmered between them whenever they were within two blocks of each other.

"Spend the day with me."

All her good intentions of keeping him at arm's length vanished. A few hours together wouldn't hurt.

"Give me a few minutes and I'll be ready."

From the kitchen, Mac heard her pad into the bathroom, then heard the sputter of water pipes. He'd already discovered the vagaries of the old-fashioned plumbing the hard way when he'd turned on the kitchen faucet. It had shot out a geyser of water, soaking him and a good deal of the countertops.

Once the case was over, he'd have a look at it. The implications of that caused him to smile. He was already planning on seeing Miranda. The only trick now was to convince her that they had a future together.

She cared. He knew she did. But she fought what was inside her, what the past had carved.

He cursed the past, the violence that had deprived her of a father's love, the fear that was even now depriving her of a different kind of love.

He watched her struggle, a tangled battle of love, frustration, and fear. He longed to take her in his arms and promise that nothing would ever hurt her again, even while knowing the futility of such promises.

He wasn't stupid enough to deny the dangers inherent in his job. But neither did he intend to live his life in a state of paranoia.

Every job had risks. Roofers could take a tumble from a scaffold and break their necks. Chemists could blow themselves up with the wrong combination of ingredients. Even secretaries had to watch out for carpal tunnel syndrome.

But logic wasn't going to win this war. The decision to take a chance on the future had to come from within Miranda. A cop learned patience on the job. Long nights spent in stakeouts, the tedium of endless paperwork, following leads that too often led nowhere—oh, yes, he knew all about patience.

He'd find the patience to give Miranda the time she needed. He wasn't kidding himself. It wouldn't be easy, but he'd find a way. He belted out one of the Top Ten tunes as he finished the few dishes.

*   *   *

In the bathroom, Miranda smiled at his hopelessly bad rendition of a popular song. No danger in his changing his career to one in singing. The thought wiped the smile from her lips. Mac was a cop, first and foremost. She wouldn't change him, even if she could.

Mac's beeper buzzed. He reached for it, looked at the number, and recognized that of the bar where he'd met Sammy. He punched out the number, not surprised when Sammy answered.

"I got something for you." Sammy's voice whined over the line.

Mac gripped the receiver more tightly. "What?"

"It'll cost," Sammy reminded him.

"You come across and I'll do the same."

They made arrangements to meet at the same bar. When Miranda appeared, he explained he'd have to cancel and made his apologies.

"This is about the break-in, isn't it?" she demanded.

"It might be a lead," he hedged. "I've got to check it out."

Her eyes flared, a warning he ought to heed. "Who was on the phone?"

"No one that concerns you."

"What are you going to do?" she asked in a voice

he knew meant she intended to get the answers she wanted.

She stood abruptly. ''Please don't keep secrets from me.'' The entreaty in her voice snagged at his conscience.

Still, he couldn't tell her. She'd only want to get involved. Too late, he realized he'd voiced his thoughts aloud.

''I'm already involved,'' she reminded him. ''*I'm* the one whose store was broken into.''

Her tart tone grated. He recognized that his male ego had been threatened.

It forcibly brought home just how much he'd let his emotions become involved when what was needed was professionalism and a cool head. One look at Miranda, though, and both became things of the past.

He was close enough to reach out, take hold of her, and try to shake some sense into her. Couldn't she see that he didn't want her to put her life in danger? That he was only trying to protect her? His hands fisted at his sides, and he turned away.

The breath he took restored his calm, at least in part. He turned back toward her and knew he couldn't stay angry. He reached out and caught a few strands of pale blond hair, lightly rubbing them together, listening to the sound they made, like silk sliding against silk.

''Whether you like it or not, Mac, I'm involved in

this thing, and no matter how hard you try, there's nothing you can do to uninvolve me.''

She didn't sound frightened, he thought. She sounded angry. She *was* angry. He glanced at her, taking in the determined set of her jaw, the tightness of her mouth, the stubborn lift of her chin. He watched as she squared her shoulders, as if settling her armor more securely around her. The lady had more courage than a lot of men he'd known, both on the force and off.

Atta girl. Then he squelched the reaction. He wasn't sure he didn't want her scared. Frightened people didn't take chances. They let the police do their jobs.

''I'm going to meet a snitch,'' he said reluctantly.

''I could help,'' she said. ''I've had a lot of experience dealing with the public.''

Mac nearly laughed. Sammy wasn't *the public.* He was a snitch. He'd likely disappear if a classy lady like Miranda showed up.

Miranda saw the almost-laugh. She wasn't going to be charmed out of having her say. The man had gone too far. He needed to know he couldn't just announce he was going to meet someone who might have information on the case and expect her to stay at home.

She opened her mouth to tell him just that when he touched his lips to hers. The kiss wiped all rational thought from her mind. All she could do was feel. Feel the quiet insistence of his lips on hers. Feel the strength with which his arms held her. Feel the love he communicated without saying a word.

Oh, he was good.

Gently, he tugged her to him. "If something happened to you . . ." The words failed to come. He couldn't voice aloud the possibilities that filled his mind, each more horrifying than the last. "Ah, Miranda," he said. "Don't fight me on this. Please."

"Nothing's going to happen to me," she murmured. "Not when you're there."

Unwittingly, she'd restored what all his lectures to himself had failed to do. Protecting her. That was the only thing that mattered.

They'd strayed from the original subject. Her safety was what mattered now. "You're not going with me."

"Fine."

The fences were back in place, sturdy, precisely placed fences that reminded him he had no place in her life, except that of a cop assigned to a case.

The thought angered him even as the professional part of him applauded the decision.

But he was feeling distinctly unprofessional lately. The lady, with her pretty silk dresses, wispy hats, and lace gloves, had done that.

She was wrong for him on every level. She was all softness and femininity, while he felt like a large oaf trampling through her life. But underneath, he had an instinct that she was special, a gut feeling that she was different from any woman he'd known, that she could matter like no one in his life ever had.

I won't be run off, he vowed.

A half hour later, Mac found Sammy curled in a corner booth. The bar appeared more depressing than ever in the morning light.

He shuddered at the thought of Miranda accompanying him. A slight grin pulled at his lips at the sparks that had lit her eyes when he'd told her to stay put.

She'd argued, cajoled, pleaded, and finally bribed with a promise to lay off the chocolate-covered doughnuts for the next month if he'd take her with him.

He'd refused.

It hadn't been easy. But it had worked.

Mac slid in the opposite side, took a look at what Sammy was drinking, and motioned to the bartender for a soda water.

Sammy raised the glass in a mock salute. "The guy you're after is called the Ghost."

Mac wasn't in any mood for games. "It's too early for Halloween."

"It's the gospel truth," Sammy insisted in his whiny voice.

"Where do I find this Ghost?"

Sammy giggled. "That's it. You don't find him."

Mac's patience frayed a little more. "You wouldn't be wasting my time, now, would you, Sammy?"

Sammy pouted. "You know me better than that."

"Then let me have what you've got."

Sammy huffed a bit but gave the address he'd picked up. "You won't be forgetting your promise."

"I remember."

His little chat with Sammy had paid off.

With another unit as backup, Mac and his partner had taken down the Ghost, alias Mickey Delaney, with remarkably little trouble.

The Ghost was nothing more than a second-class thief with a first-class knowledge of electronics. Everything about him was gray. His hair. His eyes. Even his skin. Mac took him in, booked him, and spent the rest of the day filling out paperwork.

He made good on his promise to Sammy and put in a call to his parole officer. The man agreed to give Sammy some slack in view of the help he'd given.

Mac let the other unit have the pleasure of informing the captain that the Aspen Heights thief had been apprehended. Right now he had other things on his mind. Things like a pretty shop owner with brown eyes and blond hair and a mouth that begged to be kissed.

He had no official reason for seeing Miranda again, other than to inform her that the burglar had been caught. But a whole lot of personal ones.

It was those he intended to focus on.

It was time, he decided, to pull out the big guns. With that in mind, he headed to Denver's Mile-High Flea Market. If he couldn't find what he wanted there, it couldn't be found.

Chapter Six

Miranda opened the box with trembling fingers, tearing at paper and string until she found the treasure inside: an old fruit jar filled with buttons. She spilled them over the table, gasping in delight at the dozens of antique buttons. Brass, wooden, enamel, they gleamed softly under the light.

The man didn't play fair, she thought. He had hit her where she was weakest.

It was the third gift he'd sent in as many days. First had been the fancy set of tins, hand painted and perfect for holding her collection of silver-handled combs and brushes. Yesterday, a box of old pattern books had arrived. It had been all she could do to set them aside until business hours were over.

She picked up the phone and started to punch out his number. She replaced it without completing the call. A present this special deserved an in-person thank-you.

She found him at his desk at the station house. He looked tired, but his eyes lit up when he raised his head.

"You're good," she said.

"I know." He paused. "What am I good at this time?"

"You knew I couldn't resist old buttons."

"Then you'll go out with me." He made it a statement rather than a question.

She chose to answer it with a question of her own. "How many times are you going to ask me?"

"Until you say yes." His lips quirked into a half smile that was more appealing than she wanted to admit.

She surprised them both by not immediately refusing. A smile fought for life, then lost the battle as she realized the implication of her indecision.

He stood and cupped her elbow. "Come on. Let's go somewhere a little more private." He steered her toward the lunchroom.

It was a dreary room, enlivened only by the newspaper cartoons decorating the walls. He fed quarters into a vending machine and produced two cups of coffee. "Drink at your own risk." But he set the cups aside and gently pushed her into a chair.

He placed his hands on the back of her chair, creating a sweet prison between his arms. Acutely conscious of his presence, she gave a nervous laugh.

He lowered his hands until they rested on her shoulders, lowering them still further to cup her upper arms.

All thought scattered at the touch of his hands on her arms. His scent invaded her senses, something cool that reminded her of rain-drenched forests. An unfamiliar emotion squeezed her heart.

Miranda tried not to notice. Tried not to think about how very much she liked having him so close, or about the way she responded to his nearness. Tried not to think about how much she longed for him to kiss her.

His breath was warm on her cheek, and she leaned closer, wanting to prolong the contact, even while knowing that she shouldn't.

If she'd been wiser, she might have pulled back. But she seemed incapable of it. The man was wrong for her on every level, and yet she wanted him, needed him, ached for him as she had for no other.

For years no man had stirred her senses, much less touched her heart. Why had fate decreed that this man, a cop with tender words and a courageous heart, should be the one to bring her to life?

"We'll start off small," he promised. "Dinner

someplace. Maybe some dancing. I won't ask you to marry me until the third or fourth date.''

He was joking, of course. But his words stole her breath. She groped for the cup of coffee, grateful it had cooled some as she took a large gulp. The surge of caffeine did little to restore her calm, though.

She didn't need this complication in her life—didn't need it, didn't want it.

She considered. Just because she didn't date cops didn't mean she had to deny herself dinner with an interesting man. Her own cooking skills were nonexistent. She was lucky if she didn't burn toast.

Her chin came up in unconscious resolve. She'd agree to have dinner with the man. That was all. After all, she silently argued with herself, she had to eat. She might as well do it with pleasant company.

Her arguments fell flat when she realized she would have agreed to spend the evening picking up aluminum cans if it meant sharing it with him. Because she couldn't stay away. She didn't *want* to stay away.

''Dinner,'' she said, hating the fact that her voice sounded as breathless as her lungs felt. Hating the fact that it wasn't the thought of a good meal that had turned her voice husky and her knees weak but the man she'd be sharing it with. Hating him for making her feel so out of control.

His smile was as broad as his shoulders. ''Tonight. Seven.''

"Tonight. Seven." She choked out the words, anxious to be on her way. She couldn't stay here for a moment longer without doing something foolish. Something like angling her head slightly so that her lips met his. Something like giving voice to the feelings he aroused in her so effortlessly. Something like . . .

As though he had read her thoughts, he took the initiative and brushed his lips over hers. From somewhere in the distance, she heard voices, laughter, the slam of a door. They failed to register fully, though, as he deepened the kiss.

When she felt as if she couldn't possibly breathe, couldn't possibly withstand the tender assault on her mouth for another moment, he softened it, gentled it.

He raised his head, and she gasped for breath, wondering if she looked as dazed as she felt. She must have, for Mac took her arms and gently helped her from the chair. He kept his hand at her side as he escorted her from the building, ignoring the whistles and hoots from the rest of the squad room.

"Are you all right?" he asked when he opened the door to her car and helped her inside.

"All right," she repeated. She blinked and cleared her head. "Of course I'm all right. Why wouldn't I be?" She slammed the door, nearly catching his fingers.

He grinned. "I'll see you tonight."

She gunned the engine and peeled out of the parking space, heedless of the fact that she was at a police station with any number of black-and-whites around. All she cared about was putting as much distance between her and MacKenzie Torrence as possible.

Work was a welcome diversion. Memories of the kiss they'd shared kept getting in the way of her concentration. Again.

Slowly, she began to feel more in control. It was a simple kiss, she reminded herself. Nothing to get so rattled over. Men and women kissed all the time and it meant nothing.

Mac's kiss could turn anyone inside out—although she was trying her darnedest to work up a good case of denial. Surely, she told herself, it never really happened. Surely it was her imagination that he'd knocked her socks off with a simple brush of his lips upon hers. Surely it was her faulty memory that made her think she'd responded like a woman in love.

But her imagination had never been that good, and her memory wasn't faulty.

She hoped he'd forget it.

And if he couldn't, she hoped he'd chalk it up to her gratitude for the gifts. Actually, she hoped that if she kept mentally denying it, she might convince herself that it never happened.

She had to be careful, she reminded herself. Infinitely careful not to fall seriously for Mac. Eventually she'd look for love. But not with a cop.

Falling for Mac would be her worst nightmare come true.

Not that she was falling in love with him, she hurried to assure herself as her pulse picked up its already erratic beat. It wasn't that at all.

But it didn't hurt to remind herself of the rules. Her rules. Rules that dictated that she keep her heart whole and her life her own. Tying it to that of a cop could lead only to disaster.

Once she was at home, she pushed the kiss from her mind and concentrated on dressing.

She chose a wine-colored velvet dress trimmed with antique lace. Tortoiseshell combs pulled her hair off her face. A cameo pinned to a velvet ribbon circling her neck was her only adornment.

Her head snapped up and she stared at her reflection in the mirror. Her eyes were wide, a tad confused, her mouth soft and vulnerable looking. One look at her and he'd know she'd been thinking about him. She'd never been any good at hiding her feelings.

Anticipation had done that. Anticipation of spending time with a hardheaded cop with kind eyes.

The man was too arrogant already. She didn't intend to feed that ego. Determinedly, she squared her shoulders and set her lips in a firm line. The resulting picture only made her giggle.

Okay, so hard determination wasn't her look. That didn't mean she intended to allow him to see how much he affected her. It wasn't pride.

It was survival.

She'd agreed to have dinner with him, she reminded herself. Nothing to get worried about. That settled, she felt better.

When he arrived, he took one look at her and whistled softly. "You're beautiful." The intimate curl of his voice reached deep inside her, both soothing and exciting at the same time.

She *felt* beautiful. His gaze heated as it traveled over her, warming her. And warning her not to give her heart.

He took a lacy shawl from her and draped it over her shoulders, his hands lingering there for long moments. His breath was warm against her neck, his hands gentle as they ran down her arms.

One beat of her heart tumbled over the next, the cadence picking up and destroying her hard-won confidence. She felt strange, excited, and very much alive.

The inn he took her to was quietly elegant and beautifully appointed. But her attention was all for Mac. And the way he made her feel.

It was happening too fast, she thought in sudden panic, this thing between them. She looked about for something—anything—other than the man across the table from her on which to focus her attention.

When the waiter arrived with their food, she seized on it.

"You actually eat that stuff?" she asked, feigning a gawk at his vegetarian plate.

"You'll drown in all that cholesterol," he shot back, pointing to her prime rib and baked potato, the latter dripping with sour cream and butter.

"Better than the rabbit food you're eating."

The debate lightened the mood, and she set out to enjoy herself.

The food was wonderful, the conversation even better. They argued over politics, movies, music, delighted when they agreed on something, just as delighted when they didn't.

When the meal was over, they lingered over coffee. The teasing stopped, and they grew quiet. Miranda twisted the velvet ribbon around her neck until Mac reached out to still her hand.

"What's wrong?"

"I think I like you."

A smile touched his lips. "What's wrong with that?"

"You know what's wrong. You make me feel things," she whispered. "Want things."

It surprised him, not just what she said but the way she said it. Nervous. Confused. Fearful.

The somber note in her voice reminded him of all that separated them. But right now he wasn't in the mood to think of what might keep them apart. He wanted only to show her what they shared. Together.

His mood was soaring too high, too free, to let her sudden attack of doubt dampen it. He'd find a way to overcome it. And when he did . . . A smile slid across his lips in anticipation.

The lady didn't pull her punches, Mac reflected as he lifted weights in the precinct gym an hour later. With any luck, he'd work off some of the excess energy that was charging his senses like lightning. Sweat purled above his lip and trickled down his chest as he pushed himself. His breath came in short gasps until he collapsed onto the floor.

Whatever he'd anticipated tonight, her frank admission that something existed between them hadn't been it. Such honesty was unexpected, even rare, in today's world. She said what she meant and expected the same from him.

He'd never met anyone like her. She intrigued him, frustrated him, charmed him, all without even trying.

He knew she had to be aware of the electricity between them. The air fairly sizzled with it whenever they were together. He also knew that, for reasons that were rooted in the past, she was fighting it. And him.

She was determined to shut him out.

He was equally determined to change her mind. Time and patience would see to it. Fortunately, he possessed plenty of both.

A slow smile built inside of him until it found purchase upon his lips. He and Miranda belonged together. She wasn't ready to admit that yet, but he could wait. A cop learned patience on the interminable stakeouts that were part of the job.

Patience and persistence.

He had a feeling he was going to need both in dealing with one stubborn lady.

A smile sprang to Miranda's lips as she thought about last night. There'd been a few tense moments, but she'd enjoyed herself more than she thought possible.

Afterward Mac had brought her home; she'd been too keyed up to sleep and replayed every word, every look that had passed between them. When she'd finally drifted off, her dreams had been full of the handsome detective.

She couldn't regret the time they'd spent together, not when she remembered what they'd shared, but there'd be no happy ending for them. They had only the present.

He was a good cop, both smart and caring. But he wasn't the stuff her dreams were made of. Cops, even good ones, were off-limits.

A long-held dream of a family of her own, a husband and a child full of life and fun and the future, teased her mind. They'd both have dark gray eyes and crooked grins that could charm the birds from the trees.

It didn't take much figuring to know where *that* description had come from. She scowled at the direction her thoughts had taken. So when Juan Dominguez showed up at the store that morning, she welcomed the interruption.

Juan's face was animated, his eyes full of excitement. "Hey, Ms. Kirk, I got a job."

"Juan, that's wonderful. Where're you working?"

"It's a really cool music store. I get to listen to the latest CDs, practice any instrument I want. And they pay me for it."

She hid a smile. He sounded totally surprised at the idea of being paid for doing what he loved.

"The cop did it," he said unexpectedly.

"Mac?"

"Yeah. He knows the owner of the store and put in a good word for me. Pretty great of him, huh?"

"Great." But her mind was on Mac.

Juan's smile faded, and he looked uncomfortable. "I won't be working for you no . . . anymore. My parents say I can't work two jobs if I want to keep up with my schoolwork."

"They're right."

"You don't mind?"

"Of course I mind." At his crestfallen look, she grinned. "You're working at something you love. How could I mind?"

"Thanks, Ms. Kirk. You're all right." He hesitated. "So's the cop. He's a pretty cool guy. For a cop."

"Pretty cool." In more ways than one, she thought. He'd gone out of his way to help a kid he barely knew.

When Mac showed up to take her to lunch, she stood on tiptoe and pressed a kiss to his cheek.

"What was that for?"

"Do you mind?"

He lifted her off her feet and gave her a real kiss. "Does that feel like I minded?"

Breathless, she shook her head. "Juan told me what you did. Why did you do it? Why go out of your way to get a job for a boy you suspected of burglary?"

"I never suspected him," Mac said. "I just said he had to be checked out."

"You're stalling."

There was a heartbeat of silence. Then another. Mac looked distinctly uncomfortable. He actually shuffled his feet. She bit back a chuckle at the look he shot her.

It occurred to her that he might not know the answer.

He's embarrassed. The knowledge touched her.

MacKenzie Torrence was embarrassed at being caught doing something nice. He wanted her to think he was a tough, no-nonsense cop who wore his badge where his heart should be. He didn't much like the idea that she had caught a glimpse of something more in him.

"I know why," she said softly.

His eyes narrowed. "Why?"

"Because you're sweet."

"Sweet?" Disbelief edged his voice. Disbelief and horror.

"Sweet," she confirmed. She laughed at his pained expression. "Don't take it so hard." She patted his cheek and took herself off to welcome a new customer before the horror on his face transformed into something else.

Mac watched as she walked away, a sassy sway to her hips.

Sweet.

He still wasn't sure why the word annoyed him. He only knew he'd been smoldering when Miranda had patted him as if he'd been an especially good boy, given him a kiss, and called him sweet.

He'd heard her call Norman *sweet,* for heaven's sake.

Sweet. It was a namby-pamby, weak-kneed, feeble word. It was a flat, prosaic, insipid word. It was a boring, tedious, tiresome word. Grandmothers were sweet. Babies were sweet. Kittens were sweet.

Cops were not sweet.

And it sure as heck wasn't a word he wanted the woman he was falling in love with to use about him.

"Don't," he said when the customer had departed and she came his way, "call me sweet."

"What's the matter?" she teased. "Don't you like being sweet?"

"Cops aren't supposed to be sweet."

"The special ones are."

She'd done it to him. Again. Strangely enough, he didn't mind the word quite so much. Not when it was delivered by such very pretty lips.

She pressed a kiss to his cheek. "Thank you."

He glanced about the store, relieved to find them alone for the moment.

He tucked a strand of hair behind her ear. Her skin was as soft as a baby's, her scent sweetly feminine. He trailed his thumb across her lips, courting her response.

She remained motionless. But her quick intake of breath told him she wasn't as unaffected as she pretended to be.

He leaned toward her, lowered his head, and did what he'd dreamed about for the last eighteen hours.

He kissed her, feathering the kiss along the same path his thumb had taken, rewarded when her breathing turned shallow.

Her lips were as soft as he'd remembered. Softer,

he decided. For a heartbeat, a fraction of a moment, she had tasted like his dreams.

When he lifted his head, he stared down at her, dazed, amazed, his heart thudding like a jackhammer.

The intensity of his reaction caught him off guard. He rested his chin on her head. She was so slight, so slender. He took more of her weight, nearly lifting her off the ground.

Her soft curves fitted against his own hard muscles. Soft and hard, a potent contrast.

Miranda forgot that Suzanne was in the back room, forgot that a customer could wander in at any time, forgot everything but the man who held her with such exquisite tenderness. For that beat in time, it was only the two of them.

Something stabbed her shoulder. It took a moment for her mind to register what it was. His badge. His cop's badge.

He was a cop.

How had she forgotten? His job had brought them together. She feared it would also keep them apart.

She willed herself to do what had to be done. With more strength than she knew she possessed, she pushed away. Her lips were trembling, her breathing shallow. Her heart was pounding.

Mac muttered something under his breath but made no attempt to change her mind.

He cursed silently. The wariness in her eyes was

back. It made him feel as awkward as a schoolboy, but it also challenged him. He struggled for control.

He gave a sigh that was part exasperation, part regret. She was doing it again. Pulling back. He recognized the look in her eyes. Fear. And determination to keep herself from responding too much, from caring too much.

"I'm sorry," she whispered.

"So am I."

He left it at that. She was grateful. Or she should be, she told herself. What was wrong with her? Did she want him to convince her to throw away the tenets of a lifetime? Did she want him to take the responsibility from her with a few sweet words and even sweeter kisses?

No!

She knew what she was doing. She just hadn't expected it to hurt so much. She'd known Mac had a powerful effect on her. His touch, his voice, his kisses stirred her in a way she'd never felt before. And she feared she was in danger of losing an essential part of herself.

Her heart.

She hesitated before taking a step back. Then another. Clearly, she wanted his touch. Just as clearly, she didn't *want* to want it.

He bent his head, intending to kiss her again.

Her eyes were no longer cool. They were wide and

confused now, her lips trembling. It was her vulnerability that stopped him.

''Please . . .'' The soft entreaty in her voice nearly undid him.

Whether she wanted him to continue or not, he wasn't sure. All he could be sure of was that he couldn't—wouldn't—press her when she didn't know her own heart.

His lips firmed into a determined line. A cop who'd risen through the ranks, he'd learned the value of setting his goal and then doing everything in his power to reach it.

He wanted Miranda. Despite everything, he wanted her. And he intended to have her.

Her emotions were written across her face, as clear and plain as the honesty that shone in her eyes. Fear and pain and hope. Mac stifled his impatience and reminded himself that he was in for the long haul. Miranda cared for him. He'd stake his life on it. But he wanted more. So much more.

''It's all right,'' he said, tamping down his own fear that he couldn't make good on his words.

Need swept through him in a wave. He cradled the back of her head and kissed the curve of her jaw. Would she always have this effect on him? he wondered in a daze, rendering him incapable of thinking of anything but the feel of her in his arms? He glanced at his watch. "I've got to go." He brushed a kiss across her lips before taking off.

Suzanne waited until Mac had gone before reappearing. "I made some coffee. Thought we could both use some."

Miranda tried to summon a smile, her thoughts still wrapped up in Mac and the promise in his eyes. "Thanks."

"That is one great guy," Suzanne said, her eyes dancing with mischief.

A picture of Mac appearing in her mind, Miranda couldn't help but agree. He was occupying far too much of her thoughts.

She was going to have to keep her mind on business. That resolved, she felt better until she realized she was already wondering what kind of father Mac would make.

You've got it bad, girl. Real bad.

She spent the rest of the day lecturing herself on keeping things in perspective. After all, they'd known each other for only a few short weeks. It was too soon—much too soon—to be thinking of anything more.

What she needed was control. Control over her emotions, her work, her life. For too much of her life, she had been a victim of circumstances. Her father's death and the grief it had plunged her mother into.

The teenage years when she'd felt out of touch with everyone and everything.

Now she was doing something she loved and she was good at it. She didn't need a man to make herself whole or her life complete.

She wouldn't call this feeling she had for Mac love. She wouldn't. How dare she think of loving him? So what *was* she feeling?

It wasn't possible to deny her attraction to him. He pulled her in a way that was more basic, more dangerous than simple physical appeal.

When another package arrived late that afternoon, she didn't know whether to cry or to laugh.

"He keeps sending me things." She pulled out the latest delivery and dumped the box on the table. Lengths of antique lace and ribbon spilled out, a jumbled weave of texture and color. She was already planning on how she'd use them—a bit of trim to a forties sweater she'd picked up at an estate sale last week, a border for a fifties-style poodle skirt. Her mind reeled with possibilities.

Suzanne picked up a strip of rose-colored ribbon edged with hand-crocheted lace. "He ought to be shot."

Miranda nearly grabbed it from her friend's hands. It was her favorite. She planned to use it on an ivory gown that she'd kept for herself. The deep rose would set off the pale ivory.

"What else has the man done?" Suzanne demanded.

"He cooked dinner for me," Miranda admitted in a low voice.

"Was it any good?"

"Delicious." The fact was that Mac cooked like a gourmet chef. She could barely heat up a microwave dinner without burning it. Last night, he'd served up a fettucine with fresh tomato sauce that had her nearly drooling after the first bite.

"You know what they say. The way to a woman's heart is through her stomach."

Miranda smiled. "Fortunately, my stomach doesn't make the decisions."

"What about your heart?"

What about her heart? she asked herself.

"A man who cooks for you. Sounds like he's out to impress you."

He already had, Miranda acknowledged silently. Frightened of where her feelings were leading, she needed to clarify their relationship. "We're friends."

Suzanne leaned against the counter. "*Good* friends, I'd say."

"That's all it can be."

"Yeah, I can see your point. What would you want with a man who sends you buttons and bits of lace? A man like that is only looking out for himself."

Miranda bristled in Mac's defense. "He's the most

unselfish man I know. You know he got Juan that job and that . . .'' Too late she realized the trap she'd fallen into.

''Throw in the fact that he cooks for you and what've you got? A dream man. Don't let him get away.'' Suzanne wagged a finger at her friend. ''He's perfect for you. And you know it.''

The trouble was, Miranda thought, she did. He *was* perfect for her on every level. But one.

Chapter Seven

Mac had asked her to spend the day with him, and she'd accepted.

They stopped at a local bakery and bought a half dozen doughnuts—sprinkled, chocolate glazed, and cherry filled.

"You need protein for breakfast," Mac said, frowning at her choices.

"Protein, schmotein." Unable to wait, she opened the bag and chose a chocolate-covered one.

"Those things'll kill you," he said lightly and reached for an apple from the bag of fruit they'd picked up at a roadside vendor.

She sighed in pleasure as the rich chocolate ex-

ploded on her taste buds. "But what a way to go."
She munched contentedly as he drove.

She reached inside the bag and pulled out another
doughnut. Sprinkled, this time. She chewed enthusi-
astically, enjoying the rich, yeasty treat.

He wiped a bit of icing from her mouth. This close
she could feel his warm breath upon her face, smell
the clean, masculine scent that was uniquely his, hear
the pounding of his heart. Sensation after sensation
burst through her, ones that had nothing to do with
chocolate doughnuts.

She pulled back, picking up a napkin to dab at her
lips and finish the job.

The look in his eyes told her he knew what she was
doing and understood. She supposed she should be
grateful for that, but all she felt now was resentment
that he had the power to turn her insides to mush.

She was a woman accustomed to being in control
of her emotions. Never had she let a man—even one
as compellingly attractive as Mac—turn her life upside
down. Yet that was exactly what he'd done.

With no more than a look, a touch, he could reduce
her to a gibbering idiot. Well, she wasn't having it.

"What's the plan for today?"

He raised a brow at her brusque tone but went
along. "Shopping."

She felt a stirring of excitement. "Shopping?
Where?"

His smile was smug. "You'll see."

Denver's Mile-High Flea Market was a cacophony of sound, a kaleidoscope of color, a melting pot of people. It was, she decided, a bargain hunter's paradise.

They spent the first hour simply browsing. Miranda ran a practiced eye over a display of shawls. Mass produced, they lacked the detail and workmanship she demanded for merchandise for her shop.

A box of jewelry caught her eye. Lucite necklaces from the fifties and flower-power pins from the sixties mixed with a few genuine antique pieces.

Good-naturedly, she bargained with the seller over the price. When they agreed, she paid him and hugged the ornately carved box to her.

Mac led her to a picnic table where she could spread out her prize. She sifted through the contents and pulled out an intricately crafted locket. She opened it and found miniature pictures inside. A young woman and man dressed in a style from the last century stared back at her. She began weaving a story around the pictures.

"They loved each other," she said softly, her imagination taking off.

Mac leaned over his shoulder, disturbingly masculine, disturbingly close. "It looks real."

She turned the locket over, looking for and finding the twenty-four-carat marking. "It is."

''What about you? Would you want the real stuff?''

''It depends.''

''On what?''

''On who's giving it to me.'' Too late she realized how suggestive the words had sounded. That was the last thing she wanted.

She felt his gaze on her like a physical caress. How did he do it? He didn't make a move to touch her, yet she could feel his heat.

They spent the rest of the day shopping and feasting on giant turkey legs. The day was perfect, a bright gem to be taken out later and treasured again and again.

They returned to her house when dusk had turned the sky purple and the air had a bite to it. Mindful of her nonexistent cooking skills, they'd picked up a bucket of chicken for dinner. They spread the food out on a cloth on the living room floor and had a picnic.

They argued over who got the last chicken leg and ended up wrestling for it. Mac won easily and held it over her head. ''Give me a kiss and I'll share.''

She acted without thinking and pressed her lips to his. The kiss took off, taking them both into another world. When he released her, she clung to him, needing his strength in a world that had suddenly tilted off its axis. The breath she hadn't realized she was holding rushed out between her parted lips.

''You . . . me . . .''

''What?'' he asked gently.

She shook her head, trying to make sense of her feelings. And failing.

"There's something between us," he said. "Something important."

"I need time." But no amount of time would change what couldn't be changed.

"It's all right. I won't rush you."

"We don't know anything about each other."

"I know everything I need to know. You're beautiful, loyal to your friends, and have great legs."

"That's not what I mean."

He cocked his head to the side. "Well, I wasn't going to mention that you can't cook worth a darn. I'm willing to overlook that."

She threw a pillow at him. "You know what I mean."

His expression sobered. "Yeah. You want to know if there's been anyone else in my life."

Feeling like a fool, she nodded.

"Her name was Ingrid."

The name conjured up pictures of a tall, statuesque Norwegian, tanned and beautiful and totally desirable. "Did you . . . did you love her?"

"I thought so. She was my partner. We were as close as two people can be. Then she folded."

"Folded?"

"Took a bribe. Turned out she'd been on the take the whole time. I was too much a fool to see it."

"Maybe you were just too much in love," she said softly.

His smile was rueful. "You're more generous than most people were. Some said if my partner was dirty, I must be too. It took years to clear my name."

Outrage flowed through her. The idea of Mac accepting bribes was ludicrous. Anyone who knew him at all knew he would never betray his job or himself that way. She said as much, earning a faint smile from him.

"Thanks."

She frowned. "Why?"

"Like I said, not everyone believed in my innocence."

"They didn't know you."

"And you do?"

That didn't demand an answer and she didn't give one. Another pang, one uncomfortably close to jealousy, spiked through her. Why should it matter that Mac had been engaged once before? It wasn't as if she had any claims on him—past or present.

"What about you? Any jealous boyfriends I have to fend off?"

She shook her head. "There was someone a couple of years ago. But we wanted different things."

The truth was that the man had wanted a wife to take care of all the details in his life that he was too busy to see to. She'd dropped him when he'd asked her to pick up his dry cleaning and hinted that she'd be doing it all the time once they were "hitched."

"What do you want?" Mac asked.

She took her time answering. "The usual things, I guess. A home. Family. Someone to share it with. A job that I love."

"Funny. Those are the same things I want."

Too late she realized where the conversation was heading. She started to clean up, only to stop when Mac took her hands in his.

"Someday we're going to talk about those things."

Miranda did care. She had to. No woman would leap to a man's defense with such determination, if she didn't care for him.

A sweet warmth filled him. Five years ago, he'd have given his right arm for someone to defend him so passionately against the charges leveled at him. He'd found that someone now and he didn't intend to let her go.

Maybe she wasn't yet convinced that they had a future together. Maybe his job would always come between them. There were a lot of maybes in the situation, but he knew one thing for certain. And that was what he clung to: Miranda cared about him.

The evidence was irrefutable. A cop didn't overlook that kind of evidence.

Yes, she cared, Mac thought. Whether the lady

wanted to admit it or not, they were bound together by something more than mutual attraction.

"I have to go to Columbine this weekend," she said unexpectedly.

"What's in Columbine?" A small tourist town tucked in the mountains, Columbine was named for the state flower. He'd never been there, had only seen pictures of it. The idea of spending a couple of days with Miranda was appealing. More than appealing.

"Home." The simple word held a wealth of meaning and a host of memories.

He sensed something more was going on than a simple visit. "Care for some company?"

The flare of pleasure in her eyes was all the incentive he needed. "Yeah, but—"

"I could come with you," he suggested.

"Just like that?"

"The department owes me a couple of days off. Might as well take them now."

When he picked her up Saturday morning, he frowned at the shadows that underscored her eyes. The tired smile she offered him bespoke sleeplessness. He longed to wipe away those shadows and turn the smile genuine. She'd told him the reason for the trip.

He understood the visit would be hard on her, meeting her mother's fiancé. He also understood it was something she had to do. He'd be there for her. And when it was over, they'd talk. Oh, yes, they'd talk.

He angled his head to better look at her. She wore no makeup today, her face as untouched as a baby's. Her hair was pulled back from her face, held fast by a simple barrette. Freckles dappled her cheeks and nose, glistening like golden sequins. Sun kisses, his mother had told him years ago.

With her hair the color of freshly cut wheat and her skin glowing, she did indeed look like she'd been kissed by the sun. He licked his lips, longing to brush a kiss of his own along her jaw, across her brow, over her lips.

"Hey," she called. "You planning on daydreaming all day?"

"Just admiring the scenery," he said and was rewarded by the soft blush that stained her cheeks.

Her eyes widened slightly. Hershey's chocolate. A man could drown in those eyes. Gladly.

What was happening to him?

"What are you thinking about?" she asked.

"Chocolate," he said truthfully.

Her lips curled into a soft smile. A dimple in her chin came to life. "No bean sprouts or tofu?"

He continued to stare into her eyes. "No. It's definitely chocolate."

The rolling foothill country was beautiful. Not in a spectacular, breathtaking way like the mountains, but in a gentle, more peaceful way. A palette of warm colors bathed the rippling hills with sun-baked green and chocolate brown. A breeze tore bits of fluff from the cottonwoods, showering the land with specks of white.

The colors grew brighter and the air thinner as Mac's truck wound its way over the narrow mountain roads. Trees wore their banners of scarlet and crimson, gold and amber. Tiny columbines covered the high meadows, a carpet of purple-blue that stretched end-lessly, at places meeting the sky.

Aspens, willowy and delicate, pushed their way through the denser pines. Colorado's own brand of gold, they grew free and wild.

A deer darted across the road, a blur of motion and grace. The sight was a common one in the high coun-try, yet one Miranda never tired of seeing.

The air chilled the higher they climbed; the sky, without its city blanket of smog, seemed bluer.

Miranda's breath quickened as they neared her hometown. It had nothing to do with the air and every-thing to do with memories. Memories, both good and bad, crowded her mind until she thought she would go mad.

''What are you thinking?'' Mac asked, reaching for her hand.

She jerked her head up in surprise, staring at him with what she knew was a guilty expression.

"Nothing." *Liar.* The word was probably emblazoned across her forehead.

The warmth of his hand cut through the cold that had seeped into her, and she let his hand cover hers. But only for a moment. She was grateful for his comfort, but that was all it could be.

"Are you all right?" he asked.

"Fine," she said. The look he gave her said he didn't believe her and she hurried to reinforce her words with a faint smile.

Mac frowned at her, and she quickly changed the subject before he could comment.

"The problem with this country is no porches."

"No porches?"

"My grandma's house had a porch. Folks used to gather from miles around to visit come evening. She served up iced tea and raspberry cake and the latest gossip."

"It sounds wonderful."

"It was," she said softly.

The closer they came to their destination, the more tense she became.

"I'm not looking forward to this." That was an understatement, she thought as anxiety dug furrows into the wall of her stomach.

He caught her chin on the edge of his fist and forced her head up so that her gaze was level with his own. "Do you love her?"

"Of course."

"And you want her to be happy?"

She knew where he was going with this. She also knew it wasn't as simple as he was making it out to be. Resentment surged through her. Why couldn't he understand that she didn't want her mother to be hurt again?

"I know you don't want to see her hurt," he said, apparently reading her thoughts. "But that isn't your choice. It's hers."

He was right, of course. That didn't make it any easier.

"Hey, I'm on your side, remember?" He skimmed his knuckles down her cheek.

"I remember." Her anxiety evaporated a bit, and she smiled back at him.

WELCOME TO COLUMBINE.

The sign, bearing a huge flower that little resembled its namesake, announced the town limits.

Columbine, Colorado, had its beginnings in the silver mining boom. It had all but died when the mines had given out. Tourism plus a growing number of software-design firms had infused new life into it.

Antique stores with self-consciously quaint names and restaurants bordering on kitschy promised a walk into the past. Locals joked that the tourists bought old things faster than they could produce them.

At one time Columbine had had only one stoplight.

Now it boasted three. Some called it progress; others said it was the town's ruination. The debate had been going on for as long as Miranda could remember.

It was home. And it wasn't.

She tightened her hold on Mac's hand.

Holly Kirk was petite and vibrant, her vivid blue eyes and slender figure belying her fifty-seven years. It had been too long since Miranda had returned home. Miranda and her mother both knew why. Similarly, both never acknowledged it.

Miranda hugged her for a long moment, breaking apart only to perform the introductions.

Holly greeted Mac with warmth before making her own introductions.

Miranda took her time studying Chuck Willard. Big and muscular without being fat, he was a handsome man with a thick shock of white hair and a bone-crunching handshake. Surreptitiously, she flexed her hand after it was released and was amused to see Mac do the same.

Chuck had made reservations at a popular restaurant specializing in wild game. The menu featured elk, buffalo, even rattlesnake. Chuck and her mother both ordered the latter, claiming it tasted like chicken. Less adventurous, Miranda chose beef while Mac ordered pasta.

By the time they returned to Holly's small house,

Miranda decided she might like Chuck. He kissed Holly good night, did the same with Miranda, shook hands with Mac, and said he'd see them all tomorrow. From her mother, Miranda learned that Chuck rented an apartment in a restored home that had once been a rooming house.

Mac said his good-nights and headed to the guest room, leaving Miranda and Holly alone.

"I like your Mac," Holly said when they were alone.

"He's not my—"

Holly just smiled, and Miranda let it go. Her mother knew she could never be serious about a cop.

"What do you think of Chuck?" Holly asked.

"I like him," Miranda admitted, deciding it was true. "He's funny and bright and obviously adores you."

"But . . ." her mother prompted.

A reluctant smile pulled at Miranda's lips. "You know me too well."

"As long as that's so, shall I ask the question for you?" At her daughter's nod, Holly said, "You want to know about your father."

Miranda managed another shaky nod.

The subject they never talked about had to be talked about. And in that instant, Miranda wondered why she'd avoided it for so many years. Silence didn't erase the pain. If anything, it intensified it.

"Daddy was so full of life, so *there*. To die like that . . ." She broke off, unable to continue.

Pain quivered in the air between the two women as they shared a memory, daughter to mother, woman to woman.

"Your dad was everything to me. He'd be the first, though, to tell me to grab whatever happiness I can find and hold on to it with both hands."

She was right, Miranda reflected. Her father had always said to seize any joy from the day, because you never knew when it would be your last.

And he had. He had always been the first to try new things. Parasailing, bungee jumping, he'd been doing them all before they'd become fashionable. He had also been the first to kiss away a hurt, listen to a troubled child, soothe away the rough edges of life.

Perhaps that was why she'd been so angry with him for dying. She'd lost her father and a part of herself as well.

"What about Chuck? Do you feel the same about him?"

"I don't love him the same as I did your father. But I do love him, honey. For the first time in eighteen years, I'm in love. And it feels wonderful."

"You look wonderful," Miranda said. And meant it. Her mother's eyes were bright with happiness, her expression more serene than Miranda could remember seeing it in years. There was one question she couldn't keep from asking, one question that burned through everything else. "Do you still love Daddy?"

Her mother's smile was tinged with sadness now. "I'll always love him. He was my first love. My first kiss. I had a child with him. He'll always be a part of me. And Chuck understands that."

Miranda hugged her mother and felt the last of her fears melt away. "What can I do to help?"

"Be my maid of honor."

The following morning, Mac asked Miranda to go for a walk with him.

The morning was beautiful in the way only autumn in the Rockies could be. Dew silvered the grass. The air was garden fresh, peppery with the scent of wild-flowers. Sunlight peeked through slits in the clouds, bright patches against the looming mountains.

"It's beautiful here," Mac said, echoing her own feelings. "The mountains are so close you feel like you could reach out and touch them."

"This is my favorite time of year," she said.

"Mine too." He tucked her hand in his.

It was enough.

The rest of the visit was spent discussing dresses, flower arrangements, and hairstyles. The men distanced themselves from all such conferences with shared looks of pain.

"You like pizza?" Chuck asked Mac when the conversation zeroed in on the merits of roses versus carnations.

"Will it get us out of here?"

Chuck nodded. "There's a place that does great pizza right around the corner."

"Let's go."

"Coward," Miranda whispered to Mac as he grabbed a coat.

"We'll bring back dinner," he promised.

She made a face at him but was secretly pleased at how well he was getting along with her mother's fiancé. If Mac liked Chuck, it spoke well for the older man. She trusted Mac's judgment.

The rest of the weekend passed too quickly.

By Sunday evening, Miranda felt as if she'd known Chuck for years. She said as much, earning a pleased smile from him.

She pressed a kiss to his cheek as she and Mac started to leave. "Thank you for making my mother so happy."

"It's mutual." He slanted a glance toward Mac. "Maybe we'll be making it a double wedding."

She didn't know how to respond to that so she remained silent. The fact was, she had thought about marriage. And shied away from it in the same instant.

Mac was everything she'd promised herself she would stay away from. She felt her mother's eyes on her, troubled and questioning. The tension in the room stretched taut.

She risked a glance at Mac. He returned it with a look that sent wary prickles skittering down her spine. She reminded herself to remain calm. Was that possible, she wondered, when he continued to stare at her as if he wanted to devour her?

She averted her gaze. ''One marriage in the family is enough,'' she said lightly.

Mac was quiet during the trip down the mountains. Miranda understood that she had hurt him. She also knew she'd had no other choice. The silence thickened, but she was powerless to break it, powerless to change what couldn't be changed.

Outside her house, he pulled to a stop but made no move to open the car door. Instead, he reached for her. His big hands framed her face, and a small moan slipped from her throat, the touch of his palm on her skin scattering her thoughts like motes of sunshine. The darkness of the truck's interior created a cocoon. For the moment it was only the two of them.

She pressed her hands against his chest. His heart beat urgently, an echo of the rapid pounding of her own. His breath, warm and sweet, caressed her face.

''Mac . . .'' Excuses trembled on her tongue, but they were useless.

She didn't know what she was about to say. How could she when her life had been turned upside down?

"Don't," he said. "Don't say anything. We'll work it out. Together." He cloaked his wounded pride with a wry look. "I won't ask for more than you can give," he promised.

But he was, she thought. In the way he looked at her, the way his husky voice washed over her like warm honey on a summer day, in a thousand ways that she couldn't put words to.

He brushed his thumbs under her eyes, catching two shimmering tears on the pads, then pushed back the curls that had clustered on her cheeks. The gesture was so tender that it threatened to start the tears all over again.

Tears stung her eyes at his understanding. She slashed her arm across her face, unwilling to let him see her cry. Gently, he circled her wrist and lowered her arm, baring her face.

For the span of a heartbeat, a single, endless moment, time ground to a standstill. He reached for her other hand, his fingers tightening around her own. The air hummed with tension, an awareness that she couldn't deny.

He brought her hand to his lips. Tenderly, he kissed the center of her palm and then placed it over his heart.

How did he do it? Wipe away her tears one moment and cause them to start again the next? He called to something deep within her. She felt her heart leap, then still. Her feelings must have shown in her eyes.

''Don't look at me like that,'' he warned.

Moonlight rippled across his lashes, tipping the black sheen with blue and softening the normally hard line of his cheek.

He kissed her then, a graze of lips against lips. His were hard to her soft ones, firm when hers were yielding, the contrasts heightening each sensation.

Miranda forced herself to breathe. She'd forgotten to in the last moments. The rush of oxygen into her air-starved lungs startled her so that she fell back against the seat.

Mac's hands slipped to her shoulders, steadying her even as his nearness threatened to cut off her supply of air once again. *In, out, in, out,* she chanted to herself. A woman could lose herself in such a man, lose herself and not mind the loss.

''Do you trust me?''

''Yes.'' Her answer came unhesitatingly.

She trusted him. It would have been unthinkable not to. She hadn't wanted him in her life, but he'd barged his way in and she was grateful he had.

What the future held, she didn't know. For the first time in her life, she was living for today.

''Will you trust me not to hurt you?'' he asked.

She knew he'd never hurt her intentionally. But what of the things he couldn't control?

"I need to go in," she said at last.

His lips tightened at her evasion.

He touched his lips to hers once again and then started his truck.

She watched as he drove off.

And she was left to wonder how her orderly life had gotten so mixed up. She sank onto the bed and tried to make sense of the feelings that churned through her.

She wanted to laugh. She wanted to cry. Her defenses, ones she'd spent a lifetime building, had shattered like a brick wall crumbling in upon itself. Rocking back and forth, she hugged herself.

Memories of the kiss they'd shared earlier, that unbelievably tender, sweet kiss, washed over her. Determinedly, she pushed them from her mind.

He seemed to see inside her, to all the jagged edges and raw places waiting to bleed.

Mac slammed a fist against his open palm. Pain shot up his arm, a welcome diversion from the heartache that was even now twisting inside of him. He glanced at the clock and groaned. Three A.M. and he was on duty at six.

Not that he had any hope of sleeping. Miranda's response to the idea of marriage had taken care of that. Desperation, pain, and finally fear had torn across her face in that instant when Chuck had made his ill-timed suggestion, each emotion mirrored in her eyes, terrifying him.

He knew his reaction was irrational. He also knew Miranda wasn't ready for a proposal. But he'd hoped she wouldn't react with such horror to the idea. How he'd hoped.

He was waiting for her when she arrived home that evening. Tension burned within him.

"I needed to see you." It was that simple.

She nodded, the look in her eyes an acknowledgment of those same needs.

He took the bag of groceries from her and followed her into the kitchen.

She busied herself putting away the food. When she'd finished, he turned her to face him.

"We have something good going," he said.

"This thing between us, it wouldn't have happened if we'd met under normal circumstances," she said.

"This thing between us is the most real thing that's ever happened to me. And if you're honest, you'll say the same."

He was tired of pussyfooting around her feelings, tired of pretending his own feelings didn't exist. "Come here." He didn't wait for her and closed the distance between them with two long strides.

Her eyes widened as he drew her into his arms. "Mac . . ."

She was soft. Sweetly soft. Womanly soft.

"It's time you knew how I feel about you."

He'd kissed her before. But this was different. He was different. She was different. They'd been through a lot together. That couldn't help but change them, this thing between them.

He traced her lips with his tongue, testing, tasting before slanting his lips over hers. He waited a heartbeat, giving her time to adjust to the feel of him.

Gently, ever so gently, he deepened the kiss.

Her mouth was warm. Shyly warm. Sweetly warm. She didn't move, didn't even seem to breathe. But her lips came alive under his.

He focused on that, coaxing, urging a response. She gave with a generosity that thrilled—and humbled— him.

He'd kissed women in the past, enjoyed their softness, their fresh scents, their gentle ways. But he'd never felt this way, never known such intense joy. It was more than physical pleasure, though. It was a communion of spirits, a sharing of souls.

And because of that, because he knew he would never feel this way again, he wanted her in his life.

Forever.

Chapter Eight

"Aren't you going to ask me in for some coffee?"
They'd just returned from a trip to an antique auction
held at Denver's Currigan Hall.

Miranda knew Mac had traded in some favors to
obtain the hard-to-get tickets. An annual event in Denver, the auction attracted sellers and buyers from all
over the western states.

She'd budgeted carefully and had bid on a 1920s
chaise longue and a hand-painted screen. Both now
resided in her bedroom. They'd hauled the two items
home in Mac's truck before going on to dinner at a
Thai restaurant run by friends of hers.

It had been a perfect evening, arranged, she knew,
to please her.

She had a feeling he wanted a lot more than coffee. He wanted to talk, to spin dreams for her. Marriage. Home. Family. All the things she hoped for, all the things she wanted and feared would never be hers. If she let her mind wander down that path, she knew her thinking would be muddled. She couldn't afford that. Her future was at stake.

He gave her a long look, the muted light of the truck doing nothing to soften the determination in his eyes.

Inside, she started some coffee.

They weren't exactly a match made in heaven, she thought as she set out some cookies. He was a cop, committed to his job, to the principles that made him who and what he was. She was a cop's daughter, just as committed to protecting her heart from the pain of losing someone she loved.

That alone should be enough. With any other man, it would be. But then Mac was not any other man.

And never would be.

Loving Mac didn't mean she could—or would— give up part of herself.

She'd stalled for as long as she could and returned to the living room, bringing a pot of coffee she was pretty sure neither one of them wanted.

Mac took the tray from her and set it on a table. "Come here." He opened his arms.

She was powerless to do anything but walk into them.

He held her firmly but gently. Even so, she was acutely aware of his muscular body, of the way her own softer one fitted against his hard lines. His hand splayed across her back, his touch sending a coil of pleasure spiraling through her. She arched closer, needing to intensify the contact.

He stroked her face, feathering his hand along the line of her jaw. She had the feeling he was holding his breath. She knew she was. He brushed the pad of his thumb over her lips. His lips followed suit, their touch light and silky.

His very look was a caress, and she flushed under the intimacy of it. A slow, sure smile appeared upon his lips, scrambling her pulse. She moistened suddenly dry lips and swallowed, hoping to regain some measure of composure.

It eluded her, though, as he lowered his head and touched his lips to hers again. The kiss was as sweet as summer rain, as soft as a whispered promise.

She gave herself up to the moment and reveled in it. Feelings exploded through her. Memories of the past fled and fears for the future vanished. All that mattered was this moment, this time, this man. He was everything she shouldn't want, everything she didn't want to want, everything she couldn't help but want.

The kiss changed, subtly at first, then heightening until it seemed to sear her very soul.

"What are you doing to me?" she asked, and he heard the awe in her voice.

"The same thing you're doing to me. With me." He stepped back but not before he touched her cheek and felt its softness. He was afraid to say too much, afraid he'd scare her away.

He was feeling pretty scared himself right now. His feelings for her weren't new. But they had deepened, intensified. His whole world burned brighter when he was with her. "You have magic in you."

He hadn't meant to say that. The words had slipped out. He chanced a look at her. She didn't seem upset. Instead, she looked at him wonderingly.

"Magic? How?"

He took her hand and placed it upon his heart. "Here. Feel what you do to me."

He held his breath, half afraid she'd pull her hand away. To his relief, she didn't. Her fingers felt small and soft beneath his own.

"I did that?"

He nodded emphatically. "You bet."

She moved her hand now and raised it to stroke his jaw. He didn't move, though it cost him. Waves of pleasure crashed through him at her touch.

When he could stand it no longer, he stilled her hand in his own. "You pack a potent punch."

The sound of his voice, as soft as a whispered promise, reached out to her. She knew he was waiting for a response. For a moment, one overwhelming moment, she almost gave in.

"It's time we talked," he said at last.

There was that word again.

Her eyes were shadowed now. He'd done that, he acknowledged.

He wondered if he should have remained silent. His head urged patience. But his heart, his treacherous heart, had wanted more, even if it was only to hint at what he felt for her.

She summoned her strength, pushed away from him, and gestured to the door. "If you don't mind, I'm tired."

"What's wrong, honey?"

"Nothing. I'm just tired." To her own ears, it sounded weak. Apparently it did to Mac as well. She half turned away from him, unwilling to see the accusation she knew she'd see in his eyes.

He grabbed her arm and spun her around to face him. "What's going on?"

"Nothing. Like I said, I'm tired—"

He uttered something rude. Then his hands gentled, as did his words. "We have something special. Something I've looked my whole life for. For the very first time in a long time, I feel like I can keep going. Because of you."

She didn't want that responsibility, hadn't asked for

it. She closed her eyes, steeling herself against the traitorous emotions surging through her.

"Don't diminish what we have. Please." The plea in the last word nearly undid her.

"We need time. Both of us."

"How much time?" he asked. "A week? A month? A year?"

"I don't know."

"You mean you don't want to know." He took a deliberate step back, needing space. "You don't get it, do you?" He'd held on to his patience for long enough. "We have something special between us, something most people spend their whole lives looking for.

"No amount of time is going to change what I feel for you. I'm in love with you. And while you're dealing with that, you might as well know that I want to marry you. Have children with you. Grow old with you."

There was nothing loving in his tone now, but it wasn't the sting of his voice that had her fighting for breath. It was the words themselves. "Marriage?"

"That's right, marriage."

"You're moving too fast."

He knew it. Had known it before he'd even opened his mouth. But he hadn't been able to help himself. "You're right. But I can't take back my feelings. I love you, Miranda. That's not going away."

And then he smiled, that quick quirk of his lips that made her automatically want to smile back. She barely stopped herself in time.

"You'll have your time," Mac promised. "As much time as you need."

"I don't know what to do," she said, her voice thick with emotion. "I don't know what's right."

"I love you, Miranda. Nothing's righter than that."

He stepped behind her and cupped his big hands on her shoulders, running them up and down the length of her arms. A scant inch separated them. All she had to do was lean back and she would be encompassed in his strength, his love. He closed the brief distance and rested his chin on the top of her head.

"Time," she repeated. But she had a feeling there wasn't enough time in all of eternity to wipe away her fears.

He released her, and Miranda wrapped her arms around her chest, hoping to ease the ache in her heart. There was no reason she should be tempted by Mac. None at all. He was exactly what she did not want in her life—a cop, with a cop's commitments, a cop's mind . . .

And a cop's heart.

The composite was devastating. And dangerous.

Her hands, normally so graceful, fluttered nervously. "I can't—"

He forestalled what he feared was a refusal. "Don't.

Don't answer now. When we get back from the wedding, when things settle down, we can talk.''

The gratitude in her eyes told him he'd done the right thing by not pressing for an answer now. Time was his ally. He intended using every minute, every hour, to convince her that they had a future together.

His hopes took a nosedive when her eyes clouded over, and she said, ''I can't promise anything.''

''I know.''

Life had a warped sense of humor, he decided as he drove to his place. It had given him the perfect woman. And because of a trick of fate, it had also made it impossible for her to be with him.

His jaw hardened in determination. He'd beaten the odds before. He'd do it again.

Miranda watched until Mac's truck had disappeared from sight. She'd been given a reprieve. She didn't deserve it, but she intended to use it. He'd awakened her to the joy of loving and being loved and now she was paying the price for it.

She'd been right the first time. The man was dangerous. He wasn't right for her. He would take too much, want too much—too much effort, too much energy, too much courage. He would want things she couldn't give.

Her heart mocked her thoughts. Her heart, she decided angrily, was an idiot and couldn't be trusted. It had betrayed her.

She and Mac were different in so many ways. He was a man familiar with violence, someone who dealt with it on a daily basis, whose very identity was tied up in subduing that same violence.

Violence had already cost her a father. She wouldn't put herself in that same path again. No, Mac wasn't for her, and it was time she admitted it.

When had things changed? When had his life merged with hers until she couldn't tell where he ended and she began? She knew she could trust him to stand beside her through anything life threw her way.

Could he say the same about her?

With the past tugging at her like quicksand and the future an uncertainty, she needed him. She didn't want to, didn't want to tie her heart to a man who could be taken from her at any moment.

Mac deserved a woman brave enough to risk her heart. But there were risks she'd never had the courage to take. And with Mac, she was afraid . . . terribly afraid . . . that the cost of a mistake was the price of her heart.

She couldn't give him what she knew he wanted, but she could and would give them this weekend together. They deserved that.

Chapter Nine

The wedding was beautiful.

Simple, tasteful, elegant. It could have been held in a barn, Miranda thought, instead of the stone church, and still have been lovely. For it wasn't the trappings that made the ceremony beautiful but the love that shimmered between the two people who pledged themselves to one another.

She'd had only a few minutes alone with her mother, helping her dress.

"You look beautiful," Miranda said and blinked away tears.

Holly's smile was wry. "I'm fifty-seven years old with the gray hair and wrinkles to prove it. But right

now I feel beautiful.'' She hesitated, studying her
daughter. ''Mac looks good in a suit.''

He looked spectacular, Miranda thought. The char-
coal gray suit and snowy white shirt showed up his
masculinity in a way that had her heart doing flip-
flops.

''He makes you happy,'' her mother observed.

''Yes,'' Miranda said quietly. ''He does.''

''Listen to your heart.'' Holly adjusted her veil. ''It
won't lead you astray.''

It already has, Miranda thought. *It already has.*

She pushed those thoughts from her mind and concentrated on the ceremony. Tears kept crowding her
eyes, and she blinked them away, not wanting to miss
a word of the vows that her mother and Chuck had
written and now repeated to each other.

The minister pronounced them husband and wife.
Holly tossed the bouquet of mums and roses straight
at her daughter. Miranda caught it automatically, only
realizing a moment later the significance of the
gesture.

Still clutching the flowers to her, she kissed the
newlyweds and saw them off on their honeymoon.

She caught Mac staring at her, his eyes full of an
emotion she was loath to name. If she gave voice to
it, even in her mind, she feared she would give in
to it.

He passed her a handkerchief.

"Thanks," she murmured.

His hand found hers, his fingers wrapping around her own. The quiet gesture was typical of the man. He'd be there for her, no matter what.

The trip home wasn't long enough. She knew Mac expected an answer. He deserved the truth, yet she shrank from saying the words that would end what they had.

Why couldn't they continue on as they had? Why did he have to complicate everything by asking what she couldn't give? The honest part of her knew he could do no less. He was an honorable man, one who would always put others before himself, one who deserved a woman equally honorable.

Mac had promised Miranda that he'd wait until they returned from Columbine to ask her to marry him again. Nearly a week had passed, and he'd yet to fulfill his promise. He'd tried, but she'd always managed to sidetrack him from his intention. She had a restaurant she wanted to try, an antique show to attend, a tax deadline to meet.

Because he was afraid of what her answer might be, he'd let her get away with it. He had to stop letting fear rule his actions. He could worry about losing her forever, but worry had never won any battles.

"We need to talk," he said when he pulled up in

front of her house late one evening after taking her to a movie she insisted she wanted to see.

"I don't much feel like talking now."

"Maybe I do."

The determination in his voice told her he wouldn't be put off much longer. He brushed the hair back from her face, his touch so achingly gentle that she longed to give him the answer he wanted.

Instead, she took the coward's way. "Please. Not yet."

And so did he. "Tomorrow," he said and pressed a kiss to her forehead.

"Tomorrow," she echoed.

It cost him, she knew. She should be grateful. Instead, all she felt was relief. And shame.

Mac left shortly after that and she sank onto the sofa, unable to move, unable to think beyond the moment.

She struggled to deny the realization, but the honest part of her admitted the truth. She was in love with MacKenzie Torrence.

She couldn't be in love with him. It was an illusion. That was all.

So why wasn't she feeling any better?

She knew the answer. Her head and her heart were at war. And both were casualties.

Did she love him?

Yes, said her heart.

No, said her head in the same instant.

But her heart had the last say.

I love him.

For a moment, as the words resounded in her head, she thought they had slipped out. The instant she realized they hadn't, she sighed in relief. She wasn't ready to tell that particular truth to anyone, not even herself.

It didn't make sense that she should love him, that she should have fallen in love so quickly when she had guarded her heart so carefully for so long.

It hurt enough to admit to herself that she had made the same mistake her mother had, falling in love with a cop who made it plain with every word, every deed, that his job came first.

Her better judgment told her to let him go. His passion for his job would doom them. But it felt like letting go of a piece of herself.

Tonight was the night.

Mac found her in the kitchen, a bad sign. The idea that Miranda might be trying to cook was enough to instill fear into the stoutest of hearts. Once she'd attempted to cook a roast. The piece of meat had resembled a battered baseball glove when she'd finished. Since then he cooked for them or they went out for dinner or ordered in.

He nearly smiled.

"Don't worry," she said with a wry smile in his direction. "I wasn't cooking. I was just fixing Norman's dinner."

He looked past her to see the can of dog food. He gave an exaggerated sigh of relief.

"Hey," she said. "My cooking's not that bad."

That did raise a smile from him. "Where do you want to eat?"

"How about we order in pizza?"

He made the call and then turned to her. "We've got some talking to do."

"I know. After dinner."

He wanted to protest, but he nodded. They filled the time with making small talk neither felt like making and eating pizza neither felt like eating.

When she'd stalled for as long she could, she looked up at him.

"You know what I want," he said.

She nodded.

"Will you marry me?" At her silence, he added, "Put me out of my misery and tell me you'll spend the rest of your life with me." A lopsided smile canted his lips up at the corners.

She wanted to smile with him, wanted to ease the pain she heard beneath his words. And the fear. One word from her and she could eliminate both. One simple word. Yet there was nothing simple about it. That same word would destroy her.

Why couldn't she be what he needed?

And what if she had her way? If he became something other than a cop, what would that do to him?

It would destroy him. She knew that as surely as she knew that she loved him. And because she knew it, she couldn't ask. Either way, she lost. Either way, *they* lost.

An image of her father's face superimposed itself upon Mac's.

Mac fitted a finger beneath her chin and forced her to meet his gaze. "You look like you've seen a ghost."

Maybe she had.

"I want you in my life, Miranda. Forever."

"I can't." Too late she realized she'd spoken the words aloud.

"Can't what?"

She shook her head and summoned a smile she was far from feeling.

"Maybe you'll tell me if I do this." He kissed her. "And this." His lips moved to the shell of her ear, then slid down her throat to find the delicate pulse that beat there. Sensation after sensation bombarded her.

"Now tell me what makes you look like you've lost your best friend."

Emotions caught in her throat.

"It won't work, Miranda," he said, his voice as gentle as his hands as they framed her face. Callused and hard, they shouldn't feel so good against her skin, like rough silk sliding down her cheeks. Nothing was as it should be.

She tried to pull away, but he urged her closer until they were but a heartbeat apart.

"What . . . what won't work?" she managed to ask.

"Pretending what's between us will go away. I love you. And I think you love me."

I do.

He lowered his head and found her lips with his own. Again. The kiss was a symphony of emotions, warm and gentle one moment, fiery and passionate the next.

She gave.

She took.

And shuddered from the intensity of it all.

Sanity and reason returned slowly. What was she doing, kissing him like there was no tomorrow? This was crazy. She shouldn't touch him, shouldn't want him, shouldn't need him.

But she did.

With more strength than she believed she possessed, she pushed away from him, trying to ignore the hurt that flared in his eyes.

"Don't." The single word flayed her already raw emotions. "Don't push me away." The plea in his voice almost caused her to relent. Almost.

"We can't."

"Can't what? Can't want each other? Can't need each other? Can't love each other?" Curbed frustration marked his voice, frustration she had put there.

She gave a jerky nod.

"Why not?"

"You know why," she said in a low voice.

"Because you're afraid. Not good enough, Miranda."

"You don't have any right—"

"I have all the right in the world. I love you." The stark words, thrown as a gauntlet, challenged her, warned her, frightened her. And thrilled her.

That couldn't matter. She couldn't *let* it matter.

She had no choice. She had to make her stand now. Or lose the very essence of herself. She was drowning in her feelings for him. Why had fate decreed that this man, this man alone, could arouse such emotions within her?

She was in love with him. There, she'd admitted it. But love didn't always solve problems. Sometimes it created them. Hadn't her parents loved? Love hadn't been enough to keep her father from dying. Love hadn't been enough to keep him safe. Love hadn't been enough to give him back to her.

She recognized her thinking as irrational but was powerless to banish the legacy of the past.

What had she been thinking of?

A month ago, if someone had asked her if she could

fall in love with someone she'd known less than a month, she'd have categorically denied it. But listening to the soft cadence of his breathing, feeling the strength of his arms as they encircled her, she realized her answer would be different now.

For the first time in her life, she was in love. Completely, totally in love. And she was scared to death. A cop was the last man she should have fallen for.

Fate sometimes had a warped sense of humor, she reflected. It had played a dirty trick on her. And she was left to pick up the pieces.

"What's the matter? Can't you even look at me?" he asked.

Her head came up, but she said nothing. She barely reacted at all. Mac figured she'd come up eyes flashing at that one, and the fact that she didn't worried him even more than her pallor did. There were shadows under her eyes, giving her a bruised look. He hated seeing them. Knowing he'd put them there.

Miranda was a fighter. It was one of the things that had attracted him to her. All the fight seemed to have drained from her, leaving only a shell of the woman he'd fallen in love with.

"We share a certain friendship." She winced. She sounded hopelessly prim. And totally inane.

She tried again. "Mac . . . I like you." That was worse. Insipid. She placed her hand along his cheek and felt the muscles tense at her touch.

Deliberately, he took her hand and pushed it away. "Like? Is that what you feel for me? *Like?*" He stared at her, his eyes hard chips. "What about love?"

There was that word. The one she'd hoped to avoid. The one she'd ignored.

"You don't get it, do you, Detective? I don't want a relationship with you." She heard the edge in her voice and didn't care. She was fighting for survival here. Her survival.

"Too late, lady. We've already got one." Masculine outrage rimmed his tone, turned his eyes to slits.

She watched as the storm gathered in his eyes and his jaw locked into place.

"We've spent a lot of time talking about what *you* want," Mac said. "What about what I want? What I need? Did you stop to think of that even once?"

Shame coursed through her. Because she hadn't. She hadn't thought of Mac's wants, or needs, or pain. The last caused her to falter in her resolve. He was so sturdy, so invincible, she hadn't considered that he could be hurt. Funny, she'd never thought of herself as selfish before, but it now slapped her in the face with stunning force.

She had been wrong. And now she was paying the price for it. Her cowardice had cost her and him as well. He deserved better. He needed a strong woman, one who could stand behind him, not cower in fear because of what might happen.

But that woman wasn't her.

Heaven help her, she couldn't—she wouldn't—go through what her mother had. The long hours of waiting for the phone to ring, praying that it would, praying equally hard that it wouldn't.

No, she wouldn't put herself through that. She was weak. Just how weak was brought home to her by the accusation in Mac's eyes.

She reached out to brush her fingers over his cheek, needing that bit of contact. He jerked away as though he'd been burned. Her heart shattered a bit more in that moment. Her chest constricted, and she struggled to breathe.

Concern flared momentarily in his eyes. "Are you all right?"

"I'm fine." *Liar.* She had a feeling she'd never be fine again.

"You're wrong about us," he said. "If you'd give us a chance, you'd see."

"Forgive me," she whispered.

"No." The uncompromising word shredded emotions already ragged with pain, and she flinched. He was silent for a long moment. There was nothing gentle in his tone when he finally spoke. "No. I won't forgive you for denying both of us a chance at happiness. People look all their lives for what we have together. And you're willing to throw it away because of what *might* happen."

The disgust in his voice caused her to shrivel inwardly. He was right. Of course he was right. And she was powerless to do anything about it.

How could she turn him away?

How could she not?

Memories teased her senses. The gentleness of his hands when they framed her face. The strength of his arms when he held her. The warmth of his lips pressed against her own.

Other memories came rushing back as well, scraping at her heart. Her father's labored breaths as he lay dying in her arms. Tears coursing down her cheeks as she watched a flower-strewn coffin lowered into the ground. A meticulously folded flag presented to her mother. The sharp blasts of rifles fired in salute. A dozen more images came and went. All with one message: Don't tie your life to that of a cop.

"I'm a coward. Is that what you wanted to hear?"

"You're not a coward, Miranda. You forget. I've watched you. You run your own business and make a success of it. You endured a burglary. You didn't give in. Not once. But when someone tells you that he loves you, you run like a scared deer."

Tears sprang to her eyes, hot and stinging.

Mac felt something turn over in his chest. He had no defense against her tears. No argument to deflect them. And so he said the only thing that mattered, the only promise that he could give her. "I love you."

"And I love you." His brief flare of hope died before it came fully to life. "That doesn't change anything."

The infinite sadness in her voice tugged at him. It also angered him. Why couldn't she see that life was a risk? That loving meant taking a chance?

He kissed her with such heart-wrenching tenderness that she felt tears prick her eyes again. She didn't move, simply stood within the circle of his arms and savored each sensation. His warm breath upon her face, the strength of his arms as they bound her to him, the scent of the citrusy aftershave he favored.

"I love you, Mac," she said, hot tears flooding her eyes as she admitted the truth to him. "I don't want to live without you."

"You don't have to."

"You put your life on the line every time you step out of the door."

"Each time I put on my badge, I've got to think that I'm making a difference. Being a cop is who I am, what I am. It's part of me. The best part. The part that makes sense to me.

"My job has risk," he said with careful patience. "That's a given. But it also means I'm more cautious than the next man. I don't take chances."

"Neither do I."

The deep heave of her chest told Mac everything he needed to know.

It was over.

He also knew, even if she didn't, that she was telling him good-bye. They each had their own lives to reclaim, individual futures. She would resume her work at the store. And he would go on being a cop, struggling to make a difference in an increasingly violent world.

"I have loved you from the beginning," he said.

"And I will love you until the end."

Pain tugged at his heart as he watched her turn away. Pain and an overriding grief. Her shoulders drooped, her steps slow, as if she'd just fought an important battle and lost.

Mac pushed himself.

Sweat trickled down his forehead, into his eyes. It purled above his lip and beaded his shoulders. He didn't stop to wipe it away. *Ninety-eight . . . ninety-nine . . . one hundred.* He eased the weights back into the safety bar.

The precinct weight room was nearly empty. He liked it that way. No need to make small talk. No questions to answer from his partner.

He dropped to the mat. *One . . . two . . .* The push-ups strained his already tired muscles, but he kept going. Exhaustion pulled at him. He ignored it. His arms quivering with the effort, he completed a hundred reps.

Spent, he lay there on the vinyl mat, the pounding

of his heart echoing through his body. His breath came in sharp gasps, the rasping sound slicing through the otherwise silent room.

He trembled with fatigue, but his mind wouldn't shut down. It kept coming back to Miranda and her refusal to accept what they had. He'd handled it badly. She needed his understanding, his comfort, not his anger. But he'd reacted to the hurt by lashing out at her.

Real smart, man.

A week had passed since he'd seen her. A week in which he'd gone through the motions of living and working and pretending that his life hadn't fallen apart.

He wanted . . . he needed . . . to see her, to hold her, to put his arms around her. And he knew he couldn't go to her. Loneliness clenched inside him like a fist.

He was alone because the woman he loved wouldn't admit that she loved him back. That was wrong, he thought. She'd admitted that she loved him. She just didn't love him enough. It was that last word that twisted in his heart. She didn't love him enough.

He pushed himself up and stumbled into the shower. Water hot enough to boil lobsters sluiced over him. He barely felt it. He prayed the numbness would hold, because he knew he wouldn't be able to go on if he gave in to his feelings.

He felt something shift inside him, as though his heart had crumbled. Or broken.

Chapter Ten

Miranda surveyed her living room, scowling at the pristine condition of it. She'd plunged into a frenzy of activity, cleaning until she'd darn near scrubbed the paint from the walls and the grain off the wood floors. She wandered into the kitchen. It was depressingly spotless as well. She'd stripped the floors and waxed them, cleaned the oven, and washed the windows. She'd even alphabetized her spices.

Tidy. Sterile. Empty.

Like her life.

She missed Mac more than she thought possible. The admission caused her scowl to deepen.

Cleaning house, wallpapering a room she'd promised herself she'd get to someday, she did it all and more. Still, there were empty hours at the end of the day.

Empty hours and an even emptier heart. A week had passed since she'd seen Mac. A week where she pretended that her heart hadn't shattered into a million pieces and her life would return to normal.

Doing what was right wasn't always comforting. She was miserably lonely. She was just plain miserable.

It was for the best, she told herself, that she'd ended things with Mac before they'd gone any further. It had been the right choice, the logical, sensible choice, the *only* choice.

If it was so right and logical and sensible, then why did her heart feel like it had been ripped from her chest? He was out of her life, just as she'd said she wanted, so why couldn't she stuff all the feelings he'd unleashed back where they couldn't taunt her, tormenting her with what might have been.

Put him out of your mind. With that resolution, she told herself she felt better.

Her sneakered feet squished as she walked across the lawn to collect the evening paper. A glance at the headlines had her putting the paper aside. A scandal in Washington, a sports figure disciplined for excessive violence on the field, a burglary across town and the subsequent police investigation. The story reported that Detective MacKenzie Torrence, who had recently solved the Aspen Heights burglaries, was assigned to the case.

So much for taking her mind off Mac.

She couldn't even read a newspaper without being reminded of him. The irony of the situation wasn't lost on her. She had met the perfect man and he was off-limits. The reminder was a depressing one, and she scowled again. *Dandy,* she thought. *Just dandy.* She had no more ordered herself to put him from her mind than two seconds later, she was thinking about him again.

The past days felt as hollow as her heart, the hours dragging so slowly that she caught herself checking the clock every other minute.

Memories tormented her. Mac kissing her. Wanting her. Loving her. She felt something tear in her chest, start to rip loose and fall free. She scrubbed her cheeks with her balled-up hands, swallowing around the tightness in her throat.

"I didn't know it was going to hurt so much," she said, the words strained with pain and heartache. "I didn't know." Tears scraped against her throat, raw and merciless, until she set them free.

She pushed aside the curtains to peer outside. The stars were like promises in the sky. When she'd been a little girl, she'd wished upon a star and then waited for that wish to come true. When it didn't, she didn't grow discouraged but just wished all the harder the next time. After her father died, she hadn't made any more wishes.

Her companion was cold and lifeless: a loneliness that cut clear through to her soul.

They'd see each other again, she reminded herself. At the trial. Mac would be there. They'd be polite, perhaps even smile at one another. And that would be the end of it.

Norman butted against her leg. She bent down to scratch his ears. "You're my family, aren't you?"

His answering bark was faint comfort.

She was in bed by nine, a book in her hands and a glass of warm milk on her nightstand. Though her body begged for sleep, her mind refused to settle down. When tossing in bed frustrated her enough, she rose to pace. By morning, she was no nearer finding peace in her decision.

After feeding Norman and making sure his water bowl was full, she set off for work. Yesterday's patchy layer of clouds had sealed over, erasing any hint of sunlight. An unseasonal cold snap had hit the city. Normally October in Colorado was Indian-summer warm, with heat clinging to the days and only cooling off at night.

Mist layered the morning, a wispy bit of moisture that was neither rain nor fog but something in between. It clung to her hair, her eyelashes, chilling her even through her jacket. She huddled deeper within it, remembering the warmth of Mac's arms around her.

Her coat failed to offer the comfort she sought. And she wondered how she had managed to give her heart when her head so clearly told her to keep it whole.

She arrived at the shop to find her assistant already there. Something was up. Suzanne was never early. Miranda knew Suzanne was worried about her. She had caught her assistant looking at her with a worried frown when she thought Miranda wasn't watching.

Miranda gave her a wary smile. "What's up?"

"You're a fool."

Miranda sighed. So that was it. She'd known it was coming. "Good morning to you too."

Suzanne in a rage was a powerful force to contend with. Wild hair, scarlet today, swung about her shoulders as she paced back and forth. A black jumpsuit à la Catwoman gave her a dangerous look.

Miranda braced herself. Suzanne clamped her hands on her hips and leveled a hard-eyed stare at her. "When are you going to admit that you and Mac belong together?"

When Miranda failed to answer, her friend started pacing again, her hands gesturing and emphasizing.

"You're looking for guarantees where there aren't any. You're a perfectionist, but life isn't perfect. You'll probably always argue about what to eat, what music to listen to, what movies to watch."

"Those things aren't important."

"No, they aren't," Suzanne said. "You have all the big things in common."

"Like what?"

"Loyalty. Integrity. And this is the big one. Love. Try listening to your heart. So far your head's been doing all the talking.

"You're a smart lady, Miranda. I've watched you build this business up from a couple of racks of old clothes to what it is today. But you're acting real dumb right now."

Miranda started to protest, but Suzanne cut her off.

"Happiness doesn't just happen. You have to reach for it, grab it, and when you get hold of it, don't let it go.

"I know. You think I'm a brainless twit who flirts with anything in pants. The truth is, I'm envious of you."

Suzanne envious of her?

"You've found the man for you. A good, honest man who loves you so much he'd wrestle the stars from the heavens and serve them up to you on a silver platter if he thought they'd make you happy. And what do you do? You throw him out. Do you call that smart?" She didn't give Miranda a chance to answer. "I call it dumb as dirt.

"If two people love each other—really love each other—that should come before everything—and everyone—else. A job isn't going to listen to your problems at the end of a long day, or keep you warm at night, or grow old with you.''

Miranda knew her friend meant well. But she didn't understand. Not about this. How could she? She hadn't seen her father die because of a job. She hadn't watched her mother almost die along with him because of grief. She hadn't watched her world crumble around her and been powerless to stop it.

No, Suzanne was wrong about this. Miranda knew what she needed in her life, and it wasn't a cop.

Get it together, girl, she admonished herself.

She took off early, needing to get away. The mountains drew her, as they always did. She drove out of the city and into the foothills.

The air still tasted of the city—exhaust fumes—but beneath the heavy smog, she could discern the tang of the mountains, the sweet scent of wildflowers. That was what brought her here. That and a deep need to find the part of herself that the last few weeks had cost her.

The sky hung like a heavy blanket, promising rain but not delivering. Columbines hid in the grass, their blue heads tucked down against the wind. The mountains loomed large in the distance, their crests frosted with early snow. Low-slung clouds drifted across them, cutting off the peaks and making them look as though they floated in the sky.

An hour hiking over trails did much to restore her sense of peace, but nothing could fill the emptiness in her heart. Nothing but a special man. A man she'd sent away. For no better reason than fear of what might happen.

A dam broke somewhere inside her, releasing a current of memories that she had repressed. Ashamed, she realized she'd stored away the good times when she was growing up, afraid that if she took them out they'd crumble under the harsh light of reality.

Tears stung her eyes as memories crowded into her mind. Her parents laughing together. Her dad trying to show her how to ride a bike and falling off in the rosebush. Her mother teaching her how to tie her first pair of lace-up sneakers. The three of them hiking and camping in the mountains.

Other memories came as well. She watched herself coax her dad into buying her a pair of red Sunday shoes that she didn't need and his indulging her. Saw herself as she knelt beside her dad as he lay dying. Then she saw the flower-covered grave and her mother crying over it.

Miranda let the memories have their way. She watched until they were once more part of the past. Then she started toward her car. And to find the love she'd almost lost.

Don't let it be too late, she prayed silently.

Her parents hadn't raised her to be a coward, yet

that was how she'd been acting. Letting the past rule her present and rob her of a future.

No more.

It had been a long day, Mac thought. He was definitely not in top form. A band of tension tightened around his neck. He loosened his tie, undid the top button of his shirt, and still struggled for breath.

Most of the force had returned to work, reducing his caseload to an almost manageable size. Any other time, he'd have welcomed the decrease. Now he resented it. Work was his lifeline, his mainstay, his salvation.

Those around him were giving him a wide berth. He didn't blame them. They put their lives on the line every day they pinned on their badges. They didn't need to risk them again by drawing fire from one of their own.

Lack of sleep accounted for part of the problem. His dreams had been filled with pictures of Miranda. They unfurled through his mind like scenes from a movie. Miranda wearing one of those ladylike suits and an excuse of a hat, looking more delectable than one of the chocolate-covered doughnuts she liked so much. Miranda calling him sweet and then teasing him about it. Miranda trembling from his kisses.

He longed for her, yearned for her, needed her. For the sound of her laughter, the teasing light that came into her eyes when she was happy, the softness of her lips when she smiled. All that and more.

He was a fool, he told himself, for continuing to care. Time and distance should have taken the edge off his feelings for her, yet he still wanted to see her, hear her voice, feel the warmth of her nestled in his arms.

After the end of his engagement, he'd never been with any woman long enough for her to have the chance to push him away. His relationships had been brief, superficial ones where feelings weren't involved. But life had thrown him a curve in the shape of Miranda Kirk. His self-imposed solitary lifestyle was no longer enough.

He had let her walk away. But he couldn't get her out of his mind. Or his heart. He couldn't stop himself from wondering if she was all right, if she was happy, if she missed him.

Face it, man, he ordered himself. *You're miserable without her.* The memory of the last time he'd seen her, walking away from him, was burned into his brain.

For the first time in years, he was lonely.

Loneliness. The kind of loneliness that went beyond a desire to be around people to a need for one specific person . . . one specific woman. And that woman had made it clear he had no place in her life.

Maybe that was why he found himself sitting in a

noisy bar with a couple of guys from the precinct late that afternoon. He didn't know why he'd let Jake talk him into joining them. He was darn sure the others weren't happy about him tagging along. He wasn't in the mood to talk shop. Fact was, he wasn't in a mood to do much of anything lately.

So when Jake punched him on the shoulder and teased him about getting out more, Mac turned and growled at his friend.

"You thinking about the pretty lady?" Jake guessed.

A scowl was his only answer.

Mac stared into the soda water he'd ordered as if it held the answers he sought. He could give up his job. Take up something else. Private security firms had approached him in the past. A desk job, supervising operatives in the field at an astronomical salary. For a moment, he let himself contemplate life without being a cop. The picture wouldn't take shape in his mind.

Then he tried to picture life without Miranda. He couldn't live without her. He'd thought he could, had spent the better part of a week convincing himself of that very thing. But now he knew it wasn't possible.

Jake shoved a basket of beer nuts in front of Mac. "You oughta go find her, buddy, and beg her to take you back."

"You oughta mind your own business."

Jake held up his hands, making a production of

backing off. "Your choice. But if I had a great lady like Miranda, I'd make sure I made her mine before some smart man claimed her." He grinned. "Like now."

Mac turned around slowly. She was there. Dressed to kill in a red suit that fit her like a . . . He stood there, gaping. A huff of breath escaped his lips. He wanted to touch her, to hold her, so much that his hands ached with it.

Jake took up the slack. "Hey, there, Ms. Kirk. Good to see you again."

She nodded at him but kept her eyes on Mac.

Mac found his voice. "What are you doing here?"

"I came to find you."

The words refused to register in his mind. When they did, he hardly dared believe them.

The hoots from his buddies galvanized him to action. He cupped her elbow and steered her toward the door. "Come on. We're getting out of here."

He hustled her out the door and into his truck.

"My car—"

"We'll get it later."

He drove quickly, afraid of what she might say, more afraid of what she might not say.

Miranda angled her head to study Mac's profile. His lips were flattened over his teeth, his jaw set in a hard line.

The courage that had pumped through her earlier,

taking her to the precinct and then to the bar, had ebbed. She hadn't let herself entertain the thought that he might not still want her, might not have her. Now, the idea scared her to death.

He pulled up in front of her house and cut the engine. He got out and walked around the truck to open her door. He didn't speak until they were inside the house.

"Why did you come?" he asked.

Panicked, she stalled. "I'll make some coffee." Her breath was almost steady, and her voice was easy, measured.

He snagged her arm, pulling her to him. "I don't want coffee. Let me make it easy," he said. "I'll do anything to keep you in my life." He looked at her intently. "Anything."

"Anything?"

He nodded.

He touched his lips to hers, keeping the contact light. There'd be time, he promised himself, to kiss her as he wanted. Right now, he needed to make her see they belonged together. When she'd shown up at the bar, looking more beautiful than he could ever remember, he'd let himself hope. Now he wasn't so sure. "I want what we have when we're together."

He played his trump card.

"I've put out some feelers with a couple of private security companies." He forced a grin. "You won't have to worry about bad guys taking a shot at me anymore. It'll be a desk job.'' She was silent, and he hurried on. ''I'll be making twice or three times the salary I make now. We can afford to travel. You can shop all over the world for clothes for your shop.'' He was talking too fast, saying too much. From the look on her face, he was saying all the wrong things.

''No.''

''I won't even have to carry a gun.''

''No,'' she said again. ''You're not leaving the force. I love who you are, MacKenzie Torrence, detective lieutenant. I didn't fall in love with some hot-shot security specialist. I fell in love with *you*.''

A burden he hadn't known he was carrying fell from his shoulders. ''You mean it?''

''More than anything I've ever meant in my life.''

The tightness in his chest eased a notch. Then another as her words sank in.

He felt her hands at the base of his neck. Slowly, achingly slowly, they slid over his nape, sending ripples of pleasure through him. He withstood the exquisite torture for as long as he could.

Now it was his turn.

His hands were in her hair, but it wasn't enough. He touched her face, her eyes, her lips. Still, it wasn't enough. He gave in to the need to kiss her.

Miranda sucked in her breath as his kiss ran lightly across her lips. Her heart wasn't just racing anymore.

It was tripping over itself, tearing toward the love she'd almost denied herself.

She'd thought she was ready when the second kiss came. It was just as it had been the first time. And it was nothing like it. This time she knew how she would feel, what she would want, when he kissed her. She knew, and still she was stunned.

Stunned by the force of the kiss and by the gentleness with which he held her. Stunned by her own need to give back. Stunned by the realization that nothing would ever matter, could ever matter as much as the fact that she loved him.

And he loved her.

Whatever else their differences, that wouldn't change. And because of it, she was free to give that most important thing of all: a future for both of them.

"What are you thinking?" she asked, framing his face with her hands.

"About the first time I kissed you. Remember?"

"How could I forget?"

"You went off like a firecracker." He dropped a kiss on her forehead. "I love you."

"And I love you right back." The words were as natural as touching him.

The words weren't planned; they just were. She couldn't say them enough. She said them again and heard the rightness of them. "I love you."

She'd known. Of course she'd known that she loved

him. But nothing equaled the reality of being in his arms. Nothing equaled the satisfaction of loving him and knowing this was only the beginning.

She wouldn't cry, she promised herself. Tears didn't belong at such a time. Still, a renegade tear slipped through her lashes.

Mac caught it on the tip of his finger and brought it to his lips. "I won't promise there won't be any more tears. But I'll always be there to wipe them away."

He kissed her again, a kiss filled with the healing balm of old wounds now laid to rest. A kiss filled with promise for the future. And they would have a future, she thought. There'd be children and grandchildren. They'd grow old together. Laugh and argue and cry together.

It wouldn't be easy, she reflected. They were both too strong willed, too stubborn to make it easy. But she looked forward to the arguments as much as she did the quiet times. They were all part of the whole: love and trust enough to see them through all the years ahead.

"I love you." She felt the words returned as she brushed her lips over his.